Writer on the rise —

Three years ago, William Campbell Gault wrote DON'T CRY FOR ME, a first mystery which won the Edgar Allan Poe award for the year.

Subsequently, with THE BLOODY BOKHARA and THE CANVAS COFFIN, he established himself as one of the most versatile writers in the field. All three books, marked by terse, realistic prose, and vivid, dramatic backgrounds, won highest praise from readers and critics alike.

Now, with BLOOD ON THE BOARDS, Gault has come up with a book *The Saturday Review* calls "easily his best." Moving behind the scenes in a Los Angeles little theater group, amid the jealousies and frustrations of ambitious young actresses, Gault unwinds a tense and fast-moving narrative which entrenches him even more deeply in the front lines of those mystery writers who are here to stay . . .

Blood on the Boards

"A mighty well written book with a fresh angle."
Miami Herald

blood on the boards

William Campbell Gault

Adams Media
New York   London   Toronto   Sydney   New Delhi

Adams Media
An Imprint of Simon & Schuster, Inc.
57 Littlefield Street
Avon, Massachusetts 02322

PROLOGUE BOOKS, ADAMS MEDIA and colophon are trademarks of Simon & Schuster, Inc.

The Simon & Schuster Speakers Bureau can bring authors to your live event. For more information or to book an event contact the Simon & Schuster Speakers Bureau at 1-866-248-3049 or visit our website at www.simonspeakers.com.

Manufactured in the United States of America

10 9 8 7 6 5 4 3 2 1

Library of Congress Cataloging-in-Publication Data has been applied for.

ISBN 978-1-4405-5791-0
ISBN 978-1-4405-3913-8 (ebook)

This work has been previously published in print format by:
Dell Publishing Company, Inc., New York, NY.

CHAPTER ONE

TUESDAY, he looked down at the body of a Mexican girl who'd been clubbed to death with a spade. Looking at death was something he'd been doing for quite a while, now, but it wasn't anything he could get used to. There was no investigation involved; her husband was panting to confess, and did, and it figured.

Thursday, he took the examination for lieutenant and had a lot of trouble with it. He knew before he turned his papers in that he had failed that part of the exam.

Friday, in Fresno, his Aunt Selena died.

His Aunt Selena had married at forty. She had been a plain girl, romantically unsought, and at forty had more or less resigned herself to a male-less existence. It was at this low ebb in her dreams that Sarkis Gadelian walked into her life.

Sarkis was a raisin farmer, a low, broad, and swarthy man who was trying to wrest a living from the sunny slopes of the San Joaquin Valley. He was a poor man and an unlettered man, his English broken, his full mustache a symbol of his old country background.

He was also a good man and sincere and shrewd enough in his slow way. And he loved Selena. They were married in the Armenian church in Fresno.

All the Gadelians were there. And all the Shirvanians, Bogosians, Kaprelians, Sergenians, and others who were related in any way to Sarkis. Also all the friends of all these families and, of course, all the neighbors. It was one hell of a wedding.

Selena had some relatives, too, Burkes, Hoffmans, Arnettes. Of that brood, only Joe came to the wedding. Joe liked Sarkis and Joe liked Selena. What the rest of the family thought about Sarkis, Joe could only guess; he wasn't intimate with any of them.

At any rate, they didn't come to the wedding. Only Joe came. And Selena never forgot it. Sarkis grew and prospered and died. Joe spent at least a part of every vacation at their big place in the San Joaquin Valley and got along fine with all the relatives.

When Sarkis died, again Joe was the only relative of Selena's present. And now, this Friday, two weeks after Sarkis's funeral, Selena died.

And Joe Burke, a sergeant out of Central Homicide, became a rich man. Selena had left him every dime of the wad.

Driving back toward Los Angeles, two days after the funeral, he almost went off the road twice, lost in the absurdity of it. No more petty politics. No more cadavers, corpses, or cut-up cuties. No more sneers from reporters, snarls from the Captain or snubs from the big, big wheels.

He was a rich man.

Up to now, Joe's whole economic philosophy had been based on the Department's pay, promotion, and pension schedule. He'd gone onto the payroll at twenty-two; he had twelve years of that kind of thinking behind him.

From here in, he meant to live differently. He was going to be a man of leisure. . . . But what the hell would he do with all the time he was going to have? He didn't play golf. He didn't bowl or play tennis or like movies. He liked to watch football, but that was only played on week-ends in the fall.

Well, he could improve his mind, for one thing. It could sure use it. What did he know about art, about music and literature? Yes.

These thoughts he had, driving down Highway 99 from Fresno.

In his one-room apartment on National, he took a shower and put on a robe and poured himself a good stiff jolt of whisky. He turned the radio on to a platter program, and relaxed.

He'd buy a television set. He'd buy some new furniture for the dump. What kind of thinking was that? New furniture? He'd buy a house in a real nice neighborhood. That would give him something to do, cutting the grass, planting, pruning. That would give him some roots, some sense of stability.

He had another, shorter drink and hit the sack. He fell asleep almost immediately and dreamed of blondes.

In the morning, he checked in late, so there were only a few of the boys around to congratulate him. Then he went in to tell Captain McGill he was leaving the Force.

"I heard you hit the jackpot," the Captain said. "It's too bad, in a way. I had hopes for you, Joe."

"You haven't seen my exam yet," Joe told him. "Your hopes would have been discounted."

"There'd be other exams. You aren't much of a man for study. What are you going to do now?"

"Make like a millionaire. Chase blondes and drink good liquor. See how the upper half lives."

"You've seen that, working in this town. A man can get tired of boozing and whoring. What then?"

Joe grinned at him. "When I get tired of that, I'll be too old to take up anything else. Seriously, Captain, I haven't made any plans. You know I'm no drinking man."

"I know it. And in a year you'll be back with us. And if you aren't—well, you've been a good cop, Joe Burke."

It was the highest compliment the Captain knew, and Joe said humbly, "Thank you, sir," feeling faintly like Dick Tracy.

In the hall outside the Captain's office, Arnie Jessup was drinking from the bubbler. Arnie dabbled in real estate in his off-duty hours.

Joe asked him, "Where's a good place to live in this town, Arnie?"

Arnie wiped his mouth with the back of one big hand. "If you're rich, Beverly Hills. If you still belong to humanity, the Palisades. It's got everything, everything. Hills and the ocean view and any kind of neighbor you can afford. It just happens I know of a place on Via de las Olas out there you could get at a fair . . ."

It was a lot of house for one man, twenty-seven hundred square feet of one-story California living, and it had a view of the coastline from Palos Verdes to beyond Malibu. It was too much house for a bachelor.

Joe bought it. The asking price was fifty-one thousand, but he got it for forty-nine thousand, three hundred.

Then he went to one of the town's better furniture dealers and explained to their decorator the kind of masculine and comfortable décor he had in mind.

"Nothing tricky, you understand," Joe told him, "but otherwise it'll be all your taste. I don't trust my own."

The results were a little splashier than Joe had hoped for, but it was warm-looking and comfortable and cost even less than the house.

For two days, television fascinated him. He watched the cooking classes, the antique westerns, the Z pictures, even the con men who handled the commercials. One night, he found himself watching the wrestling.

He rose in sudden horror and snapped the set off. He put on a jacket and walked to the village center and bought some cigarettes and magazines. The business district here ran for two blocks along Sunset and he covered that conscientiously, examining each item in every window like a man taking inventory.

At the liquor store he read the sign that informed the

potential customers that all whiskies were cheaper by the case. Thinking of whisky by the case made him think of the boys back at Headquarters.

It was something he should have thought of earlier, a party for the gang. A couple cases of bourbon and maybe one case of rye and a case of Scotch should handle it. He'd get some cold meat and bread and a couple decks of cards and poker chips. It should be one hell of a wing-ding.

The trouble was, he called it for a Sunday afternoon. So the boys brought their wives. And their kids. The cards were never opened and the whisky scarcely touched. The talk was Department talk and when Joe brought out the cold cuts, there was a definite letdown.

Women, for some reason, can not get enthused about super-market bologna on unbuttered bread. Joe hadn't thought to buy coffee; with four cases of whisky in the house, there shouldn't be any reason to think of coffee.

Half an hour later, they were all gone. The men punched his arm and told him what a lucky dog he was; the women told him in level voices what a fine time they'd had.

Joe watched the last car drive off and turned back to his yawning house. He was no Elsa Maxwell; that much was certain.

His neighbor to the right was having a party in his back yard and Joe saw the elaborate barbecue equipment, the redwood tables and benches. He heard their voices and their laughs and decided there were some tricks to be learned about back-yard California living.

The house was quiet except for the drip of a faucet in the kitchen. He went into the study and saw the empty bookshelves flanking the fireplace. He'd never read much. Well, that was a world he could enter without a formal introduction.

With some assistance from the local librarian, he traveled this road from Spillane to Spinoza and back. Of the writers the librarian called "serious," only Hemingway and Steinbeck seemed to be speaking his language. And though it wasn't a thing he'd admit to the librarian, neither of these two could quite match his old favorite, Max Brand.

Music, then, from the three "B's" to Hindemith, and only Chopin came through to him at his level. And even Chopin, he decided, didn't quite have Cole Porter's touch.

Then to art. From *The Stag Frieze* to *Stag At Sharkey's,* and though he sweated through a thousand critical evaluations by learned and discerning and articulate gentlemen, his artistic enjoyment was least inhibited at the Norman Rockwell level.

There was no use in kidding himself. He had been a lower-middle-class lowbrow; he was now an upper-class lowbrow.

He cut the lawn and watered it and fertilized it and watched it grow. In a Hollywood bar he met a girl he'd known briefly a few years back, and he told her about his new house.

She came out for a week-end, but she was terribly dull in her vertical moments. And he learned that sex without significance was sexually insignificant. At his age.

This was almost the cracking point in the screaming boredom he lived with. He took a walk the next day all the way to Westwood, where he ate, and then walked back to the Palisades.

In the small community park that ran along the Alma Real, he stopped for a drink from the bubbler and heard strange voices coming from within the clubhouse. Somebody was screaming.

The door here was ajar, and he opened it and looked into a small side room of the auditorium.

A lanky, leggy, and busty blonde was the only occupant of this room. She had paint on her nose and a bandanna over her hair. She was wearing denim pedal pushers and a navy blue T shirt. One hand held a brush, the other a can of paint. Her gaze was fastened critically on a half-completed theatrical poster.

She turned, as Joe coughed, and looked at him absently. "What the hell do *you* want?"

"Nothing you've got. I heard a scream."

Her eyes moved from his shoes to his eyes and she sniffed. "You'll hear more. Rehearsals are going on. Are you the new boy from the Santa Monica Guild?"

Joe shook his head. "I'm the old boy from the Los Angeles Police Department. What kind of rehearsals are going on?"

"Theatrical rehearsals, Inspector. This is the home of the Point Players. Would you like to join?"

"You mean—anyone can join?"

"Unfortunately, yes. Anyone, that is, with two dollars. You see, this is public property so we can't be as exclusive as some of us would like. You have two dollars, I'm sure."

Joe stared at her for seconds. "Why so smart, blondie? You allergic to men, or something?"

She returned his stare a few seconds and then she smiled. "No. Hello, Sam. Welcome to the Point Players. You'll love us." She put the paint and brush on a table. "Have you a cigarette?"

He offered her one, and held a light for her. "My name's Joe."

"Mine's Norah. Hello, Joe."

"Hi." On closer inspection, she wasn't as young as he first thought. She was thirtyish, though her skin was flawless and her eyes a clear and impressive blue.

She made a face. "You look about ready to pinch me. Don't. That can of paint is almost full and that looks like an expensive jacket you're wearing."

"I don't pinch," Joe said. "Are you a professional actress?"

"No. But thanks for the thought. What's your line?"

"I was a cop for twelve years," Joe said. "I'm not doing

much of anything, now."

"Oh? Suspended or discharged?"

"Retired."

She frowned. "At your age? What kind of talk is that?"

"I inherited some money," Joe explained. "Is it all right to watch them rehearse?"

"Of course, from out front. Not from here. Money, you said? How much money?"

"Don't crowd me, Norah," Joe said. "I want to look over the field."

"Mmm-hmmm. And in a few hours you'll forget your old friends. I know who you are, now. You bought that place on Via de las Olas."

"Right. How do I get into the auditorium from here?"

She pointed at a door. "Through there. Hurry back."

He went through the door and into a gymnasium with a stage on one end. Above the stage, the basketball backboard hung. About twenty feet in front of the apron, a man stood watching the three players up on the almost bare stage.

There were some folding chairs along the wall here and Joe sat on one. The three on the stage were an elderly man and woman and a non-elderly redhead. The redhead could have been seventeen or twenty-seven; it wasn't a thing that mattered.

The man in front of the stage, who must have been the director, was now addressing her and his voice was not kind. "We'll try that over. Try to remember this isn't a beach scene, Sharon."

The redhead stared across the lights. "I don't quite understand that criticism, Larry."

"It's a subdued scene. Your body isn't the major interest."

"I see. Perhaps I should have worn a tighter bra. But as this was only a run-through—"

The man named Larry raised a hand to silence her.

"We'll take it from your entrance, Sharon." His voice sharpened. *"And don't talk back to me."*

For perhaps three full seconds, the girl glared at him and then went toward the rear of the stage. The director glanced his way, then, and Joe felt uncomfortable.

In a few seconds, Joe rose and went quietly through the doorway that led to the small room. Norah was back at work; the poster was almost completed.

Joe said, "Who's that Larry, out there?"

"That's Larry Puma. He's directing our current effort. Why'd you ask?"

"He's kind of nasty, isn't he?"

"No. He's the director and the director is king. Larry's more patient than most."

Joe paused and cleared his throat and studied the poster. Then: "Who's the redhead?"

"Sharon Cassidy. Five and a half feet tall, one hundred and twenty-two pounds heavy, thirty-four brassière, 'B' cup."

"Why the remark about the brassière? Are all theatrical people envious?"

"I don't know. I'm not a theatrical person. I was measuring her only talent for you. You like her, flatfoot?"

"I don't know her. She certainly—well, attracts the eye."

"Mmmm-hmm. How about this poster? Think it will attract the eye?"

"It sure should. It's great, I think. That looks like professional work."

"Thank you, Joe." She put the brush down. "Could I bum another cigarette?"

He gave her one and lighted it for her. From the direction of the stage he could hear the voices and from somewhere came the sound of hammering.

Norah took a deep puff and inhaled it slowly. She looked up to find his eyes on her. She smiled. "Sharon's affected you already, has she?"

He shrugged. "That's a lot of woman."

"Uh-huh. Joe, just for kicks, don't let her know you inherited any money. And don't let her see that house of yours."

Joe laughed. "Easy, blondie. I don't even know the girl, and I'll probably never meet her. I'm no high school punk, you understand. I've seen a lot of girls. I was a cop for twelve years. I worked out of Hollywood for six of 'em."

"Yes, yes, yes." Norah nodded matter-of-factly. "Well, no man is going to understand Sharon completely because his ego won't let him. Just you listen to old Aunt Norah and you'll save yourself a carload of bitterness."

He grinned at her. "Okay. I'll watch myself. What could I do around here to make myself useful?"

"Don't worry about that; there are plenty of jobs for the untalented in this organization. You'll find your little niche."

"I see. What's yours?"

"I act at times and paint at times and sell tickets and make coffee and try to get us publicity and set up chairs and run out for more doughnuts and act as information bureau for great big, dumb but handsome ex-cops."

"I'm handsome?" Joe asked.

"In your naïve and virile way."

Joe chuckled. "Naïve—? I wish you'd seen some of the things I've seen."

"I do, too. That's got nothing to do with it. I can tell naïveté when I see it, and I'm looking at it. You want a cup of coffee?"

"Here?"

"Any place you want it, lover. But the rest of them usually drink it in the kitchen."

There was no one in the kitchen when they entered it. On the cast steel top of the restaurant-size range, a huge enameled coffeepot was simmering over a low flame.

From a stack of dirty cups on the drainboard of the

sink, Norah selected a pair and rinsed them out. "You'd better handle that pot; it's too heavy for me."

Joe went over to pour, and then they sat at the big table in the center of the room.

Norah nodded at the bank of waist-high windows that covered one wall of the kitchen above a counter. "That's where we serve the coffee and doughnuts between acts. At ten cents an item. Extra dimes for the kitty."

"And what do you do with the kitty? Nobody gets paid, do they?"

"Nobody gets paid. But we share the universal dream of all amateur groups—our own theater." She chuckled. "We found a place we could get, too, for twelve thousand. That's awfully cheap for this neighborhood. All we need, now, is eleven thousand, nine hundred and fifty-two dollars. We have forty-eight dollars in the bank."

From the doorway, somebody said, "After four years. That's twelve dollars a year."

The man standing in the doorway was the elderly man Joe had seen on the stage. He asked, "Is there more of that coffee?"

Norah nodded toward the stove. "Walter, this is Joe— what was that last name?"

"Joe Burke." Joe rose to grip the man's hand.

"Walter Hamilton," Norah said. "Walter's our current president. Joe is looking for work."

Hamilton asked, "Local resident, Mr. Burke?"

Joe nodded. "But I—ah—don't want to act, or anything. I mean—" What did he mean, that he was lonely?

Hamilton smiled. "I'm glad to hear it. There are so many jobs nobody wants in this organization I'm sure you'll fit in very well." He went over to bring a cup of coffee back to the big table.

Norah said, "Walter's a bleeder. If he'd given as much time to the investment business as he has to amateur theater in his life, he'd be a richer man."

Hamilton looked at his coffee cup. "That last line I'll buy. But what about my being a 'bleeder'? What did you mean by that?"

Norah said, "Give me a cigarette and I'll tell you."

Hamilton shook his head. "As long as you seem to have quit *buying* cigarettes, why don't you quit smoking?" He threw a pack over to her.

She ignored the last question. "What I meant about your being a bleeder, you worry as much about these productions at a seventy-five cent top as some perfectionist would about a Broadway smash. How good do we have to be at the price?"

"That," Hamilton said, "was a very stupid remark, and you know it, Norah. Don't you think Max Reinhardt worked just as hard on little theater work in Salzburg as he did when he became internationally famous?"

Norah chuckled. "Oh, Walter— There is a Reinhardt in the house?"

"Oh, shut up," he said. He took a deep breath and expelled it. "The painful part is, you're not really cynical. For three years you've been acting like a small caliber Eve Arden. God knows why."

She said softly, "God and Norah." She looked up. "What was the fuss about on the stage?"

"Larry and Sharon. They don't see eye to eye, those two. And now, of course, Sharon has that thirteen weeks at a hundred a week behind her. *She's* been a professional."

"*Actress*," Norah added cattily. "Why can't I get to like her?"

Walter was facing the doorway, and he said, "Come in, Sharon, and have some coffee. Relax."

Norah gulped. Joe turned to see the redhead looking wonderingly at Norah.

Walter said quickly, "We were talking about relatives, about Norah's aunt. Is it one of your peeves, too, Sharon?"

Sharon didn't answer. She came in and went over to

rinse out a cup. "Some day I'm going to cut Larry Puma's throat. Lord, what that man doesn't know about his profession—"

Walter said mildly, "Well, you were rather—dominating the scene, Sharon. Oh, this is Joe Burke, Sharon Cassidy."

Joe rose. Sharon gave him a nod and went over to the big range. "There's an assistant director at MGM we can get for the next one, Walter. I've been talking to him about us."

Norah winked at Walter.

Joe went over to help Sharon with the big pot. Her perfume smelled expensive. And her complexion was as flawless at close range as it had seemed on the stage. She smiled up at him and Joe's hand trembled as he poured the coffee. This was one of those for whom talent would be lagniappe; she projected all she'd ever need without saying a word or making a gesture.

Norah said, "Joe's one of our local residents, Sharon. He's a cop."

"Oh." No interest in the voice.

Joe looked at Norah and found her grinning at him. He said, "I was a cop. But I had a rich aunt. So, I retired." He made a face at Norah.

Sharon said, "Oh, oh. Norah's been trying to mislead me, again. Like she did with Dick Metzger."

Walter laughed. Norah turned pale and glared at the redheaded girl. "That was in bad taste."

Sharon nodded and came over to the table with her coffee. "But a fact. I'll drop it if you will." She sat down. "What a turkey we have. Who was responsible for picking this one?"

Walter Hamilton said mildly, "The Board of Directors. Of which I happen to be president. Why did you try out for it, Sharon?"

"I'm beginning to wonder."

There was the sound of footsteps coming down from

the stage into the room beyond. "Here comes his lordship, now," Sharon said. "He'd better stay out of my hair."

Larry Puma was a big man, as big as Joe, and he seemed genial enough now as he came in from the next room. "Did you make the coffee, Norah?"

"Yes, boss," she said in mock humility.

"Then it should be good." He stopped to smile at Sharon. "Are we friends?"

She looked at him coolly. "Temporarily. Perhaps it just isn't the proper vehicle for my *doubtful* talents."

He put the tip of his index finger on her nose. "I never doubted your talent."

Her eyebrows lifted. "Well, thank you."

He went over to get a cup. "Or lack of it. Let's face it, Sharon; you've never been interested in really learning your trade. And you'll probably never have to, the way you project that—that appeal of yours."

Hamilton coughed. Norah looked at her nails. Joe studied a thumb. A silence grew in the room.

Sharon said, "You—you big, dumb, egotistical—"

Puma turned from the sink to face her. "Look, I wasn't trying to be nasty. You've got what a thousand better actresses would sell out for. And you don't want to learn anything more."

Sharon sipped her coffee. "In your opinion. Larry, I've learned a thing or two since the last time I worked with this gang."

Larry raised a hand. "I know. I've heard it before. You were at MGM, weren't you, Miss Cassidy?"

"Mmm-hmm. Ever work there, Larry?" Her voice honey.

"No. I still get my checks at Sam's Shoe Salon. I will probably die trying to fit a 4-A on a 6-B foot. And you will be the Clara Bow of the frightened 'fifties. I will brag about knowing you to my few, impoverished friends. You win, Sharon."

Norah said, "Maybe Sam will leave you the place, Larry. He can't live forever."

They all laughed, including Larry. But Sharon's laugh wasn't a pleasant thing to hear.

This redhead, Joe thought, *is all bitch. But it doesn't make a damned bit of difference to me and it won't to any other male she wants to put out for.*

Some others came in after that and Joe was lost in the welter of names and new faces. They went back in to rehearse, after a while, and Joe and Norah were alone in the kitchen.

Norah rose and stretched. "I think I'll paddle home. I'll be damned if I'll wash those cups again."

"I'll wash 'em if you'll dry," Joe said. "That Sharon is really nasty, isn't she?"

"I'm glad you noticed it. You kept your eyes on her enough."

"Naturally. With a girl like that in the room, all men become—" He shrugged.

"Beasts?" Norah offered.

He rose. "Well, beastly, anyway. Like when you stretched, before. Same effect. And you knew it."

She stared at him. "I stretched because I needed to stretch. Just what kind of a girl do you think I am?"

"I haven't found out yet," Joe said. "I like you, though, Norah."

"Likewise," she said. "Let's get to the cups."

He washed; she dried. From the room beyond came the sound of the hammer again, and from the stage came the sound of voices. The windows to the right of them looked out on a flood-lighted concrete patio that held three table tennis tables, all of them being used by teen-agers at the moment.

Norah said, "We use those tables for the cream and sugar when we sell doughnuts. Nice setup, isn't it? Keeps the counter from getting jammed up."

He nodded. "Who was Dick Metzger?"

Silence, while Norah studied a cup. Then she immersed it in the soapy water. "Why do you want to know?"

"Just nosy, I suppose. When Sharon mentioned that name, I happened to be looking at you. God, you looked—bleak."

"You still have to play detective, do you?" Her voice was low.

"I'm sorry."

"Don't be. He was a—a dilettante. He dabbled in art and music and literature—and gullible blondes. He was a very charming, very wealthy, very useless tall and handsome gentleman who drove his Jaguar over the cliff on Chautauqua three years ago."

"Accident?"

"I suppose."

"He died?"

"Immediately."

Joe put a hand on Norah's forearm. "Serious, huh?"

She was motionless. "I guess it was, Joe." She took a deep breath. "It wasn't until he died that we learned he had a wife."

CHAPTER TWO

NORAH LEFT SOON AFTER THAT, and Joe went back in to watch the rehearsal. They were working on a different scene, and Walter Hamilton sat in one of the chairs along the wall.

Joe went over to sit next to him.

Walter whispered, "I've been thinking about a job for you, and I know one you can do tomorrow. Someone has to take our placards and posters out to the merchants around town. Would you do that?"

Joe nodded. "I'd be glad to. I suppose, the way Sharon and Larry Puma are getting along, one of them will quit the play."

Hamilton shook his head. "Larry won't. And we need Sharon; she *does* bring the customers in. So we'll coddle her." He rubbed the back of his neck wearily. "Four years of headaches for a net of forty-eight dollars. Why do we do it, Joe?"

Joe shrugged. "I'm a Johnny-come-lately, so I don't know, yet. But it's kind of—oh, magic, maybe?"

"Illusion," Walter said. "Like any art. Or like—living. I guess we'd all cut our throats if it wasn't for our illusions."

Joe smiled. "Speak for yourself. I've been a cop too long to have any."

"I see." Hamilton looked at Joe and back at the stage. "You seem to have instilled some in Norah. She showed more interest, tonight, than she has in any male for years. She's a really fine girl, that Norah Payne, Joe."

Was it a warning? Joe said, "She seems very nice."

"She is very nice. But she's the kind of woman who isn't complete without a man."

"Like Sharon?"

Hamilton shook his head. "Sharon doesn't need men; she needs what they can do for her. Do you want to pick up those placards at my house, or shall I bring them to yours?"

Joe rose. "I'll pick 'em up."

"All right. It's 19040 Bollinger Drive. I won't be home after eight in the morning, but someone there will give them to you. Welcome to the Players, Joe."

"Thanks. I think I'm going to enjoy it."

Walking home, Joe had a sense of belonging to a community for the first time since high school. It was one of those rare freaks of weather for California, a warm night, the wind coming from the desert. He stood for a moment in the little park across from his house and looked out at the lights of the Santa Monica Bay.

He thought of Norah, but the thought of Sharon crowded Norah from his mind. A tramp she might be, but even Larry Puma had to admit her attraction was immense.

And how did he know she was a tramp? A girl with her face and figure is going to be resented early in life by other girls. And if she has any spirit, she is going to learn to protect herself with the weapons women use on others, a sharp tongue.

And Puma could be wrong about her talent. It didn't figure that a shoe salesman should know more about theatrical talent than MGM. It didn't figure right to Joe.

At the time.

It was only ten o'clock and he wasn't tired. He turned on his television set, but there wasn't a drama to be found. He snapped it off and went into the study.

His new books stared back at him; his record player stood mutely against the north wall. Through the full-length windows he could see his walled and brick-floored patio. He'd have a party out there for the gang when he got to know them better. And no bologna on unbuttered bread; Sharon could help him plan it.

In high school, in his junior year, he'd been pressured by the drama teacher into playing the part of a college football player, a loud and extroverted character who got his come-uppance in the end.

The school paper had called him "more than adequate" in the role. The drama teacher had overlooked him in subsequent productions, but she was a busy woman. And perhaps because he'd protested so much about his initial appearance she did not have the incentive to force him further.

He stood now, seeing his image in the full-length windows, trying to remember some movie cops he'd sneered at through the years.

He took a deep breath and faced his image squarely. "Look," he said hoarsely, "so she's a tramp, huh? So she's mine, too. Just keep your tongue and your hands off her, understand?"

It wasn't exactly Bogart, but he'd seen worse. Maybe it would be better to underplay it, like those Limeys. He composed his face and lifted his eyebrows sightly.

"I know she's no angel, of course. But that's not *your* concern. Because, you see, she's mine—*all mine.*"

No, no, no. He wasn't thin enough and superior enough to give that any punch. Let's see, maybe Dana Andrews like, casual and with undertones. He put a hand in his pocket and smiled wryly.

"We understand each other. Morals?" A chuckle. "I'm not concerned with her morals and I'm sure she isn't. What makes them your business?"

He wasn't the most objective critic in the world, but even he had to admit he hadn't quite brought it off. Well, somebody had to sell the doughnuts and take the signs around and wash the coffee cups.

He took the signs around next morning. The signs stated that *A KISS FOR KATE*, a three-act play by Roney Scott, would be presented by the Point Players at the Playhouse on Thursday, Friday, and Saturday, March 5th to March 7th, inclusive. Admission was only seventy-five cents. All seats.

The merchants were surprisingly agreeable about giving him space in their windows. But after covering all the realtors and filling stations, the two jewelers, both weekly papers, the specialty shops, he still had over a dozen cards left.

Four of these he placed in super-markets in Santa Monica. That should give him a maximum of coverage for a minimum of distribution. The others he placed as strategically as possible in Malibu and Topanga. The posters Norah had painted were for prearranged distribution in focal points in these communities.

Driving back from Malibu, he had to stop for some bathers who were crossing the road, walking to the beach from their car, which was parked on the east side of the highway.

The girl was Sharon Cassidy. The man with her was older, about fifty, tall and slim. The car he'd parked was a new one, a big Chrysler convertible.

In his '47 Chev, Joe sat quietly, hoping she wouldn't look his way. Because the chances were she'd snub him, seeing the car, and though it was a thing he knew, it wasn't a thing he wanted to find out.

She didn't look beyond the radiator ornament. Driving away, Joe tried to analyze the stupidity of his reasoning. Didn't he have any pride, any dignity? What the hell was it to him what she thought of him, a girl who judged everything and everybody only by the possible advantage to herself?

She means to me, he thought, *just what she probably means to that ageing wolf she's with. Only oftener, because I'm younger.*

He had no illusions about girls like Sharon. He kept telling himself.

But there wasn't any sensible reason why a man of his means should drive a '47 car. It looked silly sitting in front of a fifty-thousand-dollar house. The least he should do was get a new Chev or Ford or Plymouth.

He went into Santa Monica that afternoon and bought a new Chrysler convertible, a duplicate, except for color, of the car he'd seen parked on the Pacific Coast Highway that morning.

When he brought it home, he considered leaving it in the driveway at first. But that, he realized, was infantile exhibitionism; he drove it into the garage.

He was frying some eggs when his phone rang. It was Norah. "Did I see you driving a new Chrysler past our office about ten minutes ago?"

"I've got one. Where's your office?"

"On Sunset. I work for the Point Realty Company. Would you like to buy a house?"

"I bought one. Hey, why don't we go to the beach?"

"That isn't why I called. Walter told me you're taking the signs around, and I wanted you to know the posters are ready."

"I'll get 'em. You don't want to go to the beach?"

"I shouldn't. I'm supposed to show a house at five o'clock."

"I see. It wouldn't be good business to put it off?"

A pause. "They aren't going to buy, I'm almost sure. And any of the other salesmen could show it. I— That's certainly an impressive car you bought, mister."

"Then we could go to dinner," Joe suggested. "And

maybe a show or something? It's a beautiful day, blondie."

"I know, I know. All right, I'm sold. Pick me up at my apartment in forty-five minutes." She gave him the address.

It was an apartment house on Sunset, and she was ready and waiting in front when he drove up. She stood on the curb a moment, admiring the car while Joe admired her.

She had a slim, beautifully proportioned figure and the plain black swim suit she wore was in effective contrast to her wheat-blond hair. Emotion stirred in Joe. Their eyes met and he saw the challenge in hers.

"Beautiful," she said. "It's beautiful."

"You, too." He opened the door on the curb side.

"Stop leering," she said. "You look like you're going to eat me." She slid in and closed the door. "Isn't it a great day?"

"Unusual. Any place along the beach you prefer, particularly?"

"Uh-uh. You pick one. When did you buy this?"

He swung in a U turn and headed west on Sunset. "About an hour ago. Kind of showy, isn't it, for a flatfoot?"

"You're not a flatfoot. You're a—patron of the arts. Joe you're not just going crazy, are you? You should have hired a business manager, probably."

"Probably, but I haven't gone crazy yet. I didn't pay the asking price on that house, for one thing."

"You think. What did you pay?"

"Forty-nine thousand, three hundred."

"Joe—*no!*"

He glanced at her wonderingly. "Norah, yes. Why?"

She shook her head. "It has been going begging for three months. At *forty-one thousand dollars.*"

He said, "And a cop buddy of mine was a participating agent in the deal."

"And you talked to the principals, the sellers?"

"The realtor owned it. I bought it from him."

"Oh, yes. Oh, indeed. He bought it as soon as he knew you were hooked. And made himself a quick eight thousand dollars on top of his commission. That was Deutscher, wasn't it?"

"That's the man. He's in the Swarthmore Patio Building."

"I know him. And I think you'll be getting a refund, Joe. Or Mr. Deutscher will go up in front of the Board. That's highly unethical, you know."

They were at the foot of Sunset now, and Joe turned right on the Pacific Coast Highway. He said, "I should have hired you as my business manager. You'd have saved me eight thousand, right off."

Cars were parked on both sides of the highway here. They drove on to where the parked cars were sparser. And there, on the bend, was the Chrysler. Joe slid his car in behind it.

It was after three now, and the sun was hidden by the cliff towering above them. But the beach was in the full glare of it and the red hair of Sharon Cassidy like a beacon on the white sand.

They had to wait for traffic before they could cross the road, and Joe noticed Norah's roving glance pause for a moment when it came to the red hair. Her eyes narrowed.

"Isn't that—Sharon, there?"

"Sharon? Sharon who—? Oh, you mean that redhead?"

Norah turned to face him. "Cut it out. Look, mister, you didn't plan a— No, of course not. How could you?"

"We can get across now," Joe said mildly. "Unless it *is* Sharon, and you don't want to stop here?"

"Don't be silly. It was a random, senseless suspicion I had. I know you're not sly, Joe."

He took her arm. "Thank you."

The thin man was lying full-length on the sand; Sharon

sat next to him, eating a hot dog. A *Theatre Arts* magazine was open in her lap. The thin man, they saw as they
drew closer, was asleep, the peak of a jockey cap shading
his eyes.

Sharon looked up and smiled. "Well, welcome to the
sun. I could use some company. My—friend finds me dull,
I guess."

Norah spread the blanket she'd brought. "Put him in
alcohol; he's the only specimen of his kind I've ever met."

The thin man mumbled in his sleep.

Norah asked, "Is he the assistant director at MGM?"

Sharon shook her head. "He's a producer at Paramount.
Bruce Dysart, his name is. If he'd wake up, I could intro-
duce you."

"I can wait," Norah said. "That hot dog reminds me
I missed lunch. How are you fixed for funds, Joe?"

"I can swing it," Joe said. He looked at Sharon. "Could
I get you something?"

"Another Coke, if you would. And a candy bar, if there
are any that look reasonably new."

"And a comic book?" Norah suggested. "You've made
your point with that *Theatre Arts*, now."

"I've read this magazine since I was twelve years old,
Miss Payne. You can believe that or not; I don't give the
tiniest damn, either way."

"I'll get the stuff," Joe said, and got out of there.

When he came back with a box full of Cokes and sand-
wiches and candy bars, Dysart had joined the living. He
was reclining on one elbow, and he acknowledged Sharon's
introduction with a casual wave of his free hand.

Sharon was saying, "Bruce thinks like Larry Puma does;
all I have is the body. Only Bruce tells me bodies are eight
cents a dozen in Hollywood." She looked at Joe. "What
do you think of that?"

"There are a lot of beautiful bodies without attraction,"
Joe said. "At least they don't attract me. But I think

you've got what—well, Jean Harlow had. Nobody's had it since." He paused. "For me, anyway."

Dysart yawned. "You might be right. And you might not be. Nobody in the industry is spending speculative money right now. And let's face it, Sharon, you would be highly speculative."

Norah munched on a sandwich and looked smug. Dysart reached out for a Coke. Joe sat facing them, his back to the water.

Sharon said, "I wouldn't be speculative in a small part in a picture already scheduled to be shot."

Dysart closed his eyes. "Where *do* you get your information? You're talking about *Week End Widow,* aren't you?"

"Mmmm-hmmm." Sharon looked at him candidly.

"That isn't scheduled for production—yet. Who told you about it?"

"A birdie. A little birdie."

Dysart was looking grim. "A big birdie with horn-rimmed glasses. You've been spending some time with him, haven't you? I'll take care of him."

Sharon smiled. "Who'll take care of me? Just because you're trying to beat down the price of the book, you want to keep it a secret. Think of the poor author."

"Think of him if we don't produce it. Nobody else will, nobody worth-while. Only because his agent's a highway robber, we've had to play this kind of game. And loose talk could ruin it all around—for all concerned."

Sharon yawned. "I suppose. I'd better shut up about it, huh? Isn't there even a teenie part you haven't cast?"

Dysart studied her for seconds. "Is this—blackmail?"

Norah said, "Hasn't anyone something pleasant to say about here? This is awfully grim talk for such a beautiful day."

Dysart looked at Norah and smiled. "You're right. I'm sorry. I apologize. Sharon brings out the—worst in me."

"That's the attraction I meant," Joe put in. "She's got it."

Norah and Dysart laughed. Sharon's laugh came in a little later and she looked at Joe speculatively when she'd finished.

Then Dysart rose to a crouch and started to pick up his towel and sun glasses. He stood up and slid into his loafers. "Well, we'll have to be leaving you people. I've an important engagement at five o'clock."

Sharon rose, too, her manner distant, her face grave and thoughtful. Then she seemed to shake the mood, for she smiled at Joe and Norah. "See you at rehearsal. Be good."

Joe stood, watching them walk off. Then he looked down to find Norah watching him.

Norah said, "You like that, don't you?"

Joe shrugged. "I like you. What do you think of this Dysart?"

"Fine man. He lives in our little village, you know, not too far from the clubhouse. He's the wrong man for Sharon to cross. He could blacklist her in every studio in town."

"Not if he's a fine man."

"*Because* he is. He really owes it to the industry. Let's not talk about Sharon this afternoon. Incidentally, you didn't know she was here, by any chance, did you?"

Joe didn't hesitate before shaking his head. "How would I know that?" He flopped down on the sand next to her. "How come a girl of your all-around charm is single?"

"I was divorced seven years ago from a man who preferred Cedar Rapids."

"Seven years ago? Were you old enough to be married seven years ago?"

"That line is phony. We'll take it again from where you dropped to the sand."

Joe picked up a handful of sand and studied it. "You're so—oh, comfortable."

"Thank you. I forgot my knitting this afternoon, and

my bifocals. Is that the best you can do?"

"Well, you've got a beautiful figure and a lovely face and a quick, interesting mind."

"But I don't bring out the worst in you, eh?"

"Not yet. Do you want to?"

"Not yet." She rummaged in the box he'd brought. "There's a dog left and a candy bar. Take your choice."

"I'm not hungry. That Dysart sure looked grim when he left here. I wonder who the man with the horn-rimmed glasses is, the one who leaked the story?"

"I don't know. Whoever he is, the ax will fall, I'll bet."

"Sure. That's some jungle, that movie world. I had plenty of cases among that gang."

"You saw the wrong end of it, working for the Department, Joe. There are a lot of fine people in the industry. Only they don't get the publicity the café brawlers and legalized sex addicts do."

"You sound like Gerta Gabbler, now. I read her column, too."

"I don't. Let's not fight. It's too nice a day. You wouldn't have a cigarette on you, would you? I seem to have come away without mine."

Joe laughed and she laughed and the sun was there and the quiet, shining water; they relaxed. It was a pleasant afternoon and they topped it with a fine meal, later, at a steak house in the Santa Monica Canyon.

It was too nice a night to waste indoors; they drove up the coast, after that, and had a few drinks at Pierre's Pier, beyond Malibu.

Joe let Norah drive, coming home, and she was like a kid with a new electric train. When she pulled to the curb, in front of her apartment building, she told him, "As your business manager, I think you made a wise investment. Thanks for a wonderful day."

"Thank you." He stared at her in the glow from a street lamp.

She stared back mockingly. "Save that look for Sharon. I'm not that easy." She patted his cheek. "Don't forget those posters tomorrow."

"I won't. And you don't need to keep your guard up. I'm kind of a gentleman."

"It's gentlemen I'm vulnerable to. Good night, Joe. Watch your money, won't you?"

He nodded. "Good night."

Driving home, he reflected that he'd had a very enjoyable day. All because he'd stopped to have a drink at the bubbler next to the playground clubhouse yesterday afternoon. He'd never been a joiner, except for a brief membership in the American Legion, but joining the Point Players had certainly been a bright move.

He thought of Norah and wondered what the husband from Cedar Rapids had been like and the dilettante who'd driven his Jaguar over the cliff. It didn't seem likely those had been the only men in her life.

He fell asleep thinking of her, but dreamed of Sharon.

In the morning, in the *Chronicle,* Gerta Gabbler had it in her column:

Though the author may not know it, Bruce Dysart Productions is all ready to go on the shooting of Dial Forest's best seller, Week End Widow. *Though negotiations are still going on over the purchase price of the book, Dysart has made some private commitments regarding the casting of it. Shenanigans?*

Joe thought of the scene on the beach yesterday, and wondered if Sharon had given Gerta this beat. This column was probably written before yesterday afternoon, though; if Sharon had planned to use the information as a weapon, she wouldn't have given it to Gerta before yesterday afternoon.

If there'd been one leak, there could be others. Including the big bird with the horn-rimmed glasses.

He ate breakfast at the drugstore and took the posters around to the key points in the village they were assigned to. Then he stopped in at the Point Realty Company and Norah was there, at a desk in the rear of the huge room.

She waved him over.

He took a seat in the chair on the opposite side of her desk. "Did you read Gerta Gabbler this morning?"

"I never read Gerta Gabbler."

"Well, that business is in there, about casting the show without letting the author know. You remember—"

"I remember. And who cares?" She slid a check across the desk toward him. "I've been doing a little blackmail myself, this morning."

It was a check for three thousand dollars, made out to Joe Burke and signed by August Deutscher.

Deutscher was the participating realtor in the sale of the house he'd bought. Joe looked at the check and back at Norah. "What gives?"

"Augie claims they bought the place for forty-three thousand, three hundred and he split that, and the commission, with this friend of yours. This would be half, but I think he's lying."

"And what have you got on him?"

"Enough to lose him his license. I'll get after your friend, too."

Joe shook his head and shoved the check back. "So they pulled a cute one on me. I should pay for being that dumb, for not checking with the original sellers and not finding out about real-estate values out here. I deserved to get stung."

"Joe Burke, don't be so stupid. Of all the nouveau-riche vulgarities I ever heard, that was the dullest. Take this check. And deposit it."

"If you'll take half, for collecting."

"I won't take a dime from you, Joe Burke. Don't patronize me."

He grinned at her. "Proud, aren't you? Norah, what Augie pulled goes on all the time. I know."

"Not in the Palisades. That, *I* know."

He picked up the check. "All right. But couldn't I buy you a lunch, at least? It's about that time."

She glanced at the clock on the wall. "All right. But try and act like a nice, stupid Irish cop and not some loud and vulgar millionaire."

"Easy, lady. You want Nixon to investigate you?"

"That's better. Do you like Chinese food?"

"Mmmm-hmm," he lied. "Let's go."

The restaurant was only a few doors from the Point Realty office and there was American food on the menu. But Norah wanted the Special and if two ordered that, there were added dishes.

He was glad he'd been a gentleman. For though the food was standard Chinese fare, the cooking of it wasn't. He had egg fooyoung and sweet, sour pork, fried shrimp and fried rice and chow mein and spare ribs. Every mouthful was a delight.

She smiled as he finished. "I'll ask you again—do you like Chinese food?"

"I do now. I was lying before."

"I knew it. You're a transparent liar. And don't lie to me, Joe. Not even about a silly thing like this."

"Don't sound so serious, blondie. Is it that important to you, my lying?"

"It is. Joe, you are one of the most—*genuine* people I've met in a long time. Stay the way you are."

He offered her a cigarette. "You've sort of taken me over, haven't you? Worrying about my money, and all. Warning me against poor little Sharon and tackling Deutscher. Is it the mother instinct in you?"

"It must be," she said. "Well, I've a house to show at one-thirty. I'd better get back."

"It's not even one o'clock, yet."

"I know. But I've some other work to do first."

He stood up. "You lie even worse than I do. Let's go."

He walked back to the office with her and then drove over to the local branch library.

The librarian said, "I haven't seen you for quite a while, Mr. Burke. Did you give up your planned reading program?"

He nodded humbly. "I wasn't getting anywhere with it. What have you on the theater, amateur theater?"

She took him over to a shelf behind her desk. "Quite a lot for a small library. And if there are any you'd like, let me know and I can order them from the main library." She seemed about to say more but evidently decided against it.

She'd been eager to co-operate in his reading orgy of a few months back; Joe sensed that a word from him would start her all over again.

He picked three volumes from the shelf she'd shown him and checked them out. At the desk, she said, "We have Hemingway's latest—*The Old Man and the Sea*. Remember, you did like Mr. Hemingway."

Joe grinned at her. "Okay, I'm sold. Is it a good one?"

"His best. And there's a new— Oh, I mustn't rush you. I'll tell you about that when you've finished the Hemingway."

He finished the Hemingway around four o'clock. For once, he could agree completely with the librarian. This was the kind of powerful, clean, and simple language he could understand. This was one man he'd have to rank above Max Brand.

He didn't open the other books; he put on a pair of trunks and went down to the beach for the scant hour of sunshine that was left.

He took a shower when he came back and fried himself a couple eggs and then lay down for a nap. It was after eight when he wakened, and rehearsal was scheduled for eight-thirty.

When he came around the walk from the parking lot, ten minutes later, he could see Norah, Sharon, and Walter Hamilton in the kitchen. He headed for that door.

As he came in, Sharon was saying, "—and he seems to think I'm responsible. So I told him I'd be here tonight, and he said he was coming over to talk to me." She looked toward the door. "Good evening, Joe."

"Hi. Are you talking about Bruce Dysart, by any chance?"

"That's right. The man's gone insane. He threatens to get revenge on everybody who had anything to do with the leak. Bruce isn't what I'd call a really reasonable man."

Joe closed the door and nodded at Walter and Norah. "We'll protect our star, won't we?"

Norah looked at him blankly. Walter said, "If he isn't armed. I'm no good against a gun."

Sharon laughed. "I'm sure Bruce wouldn't know what to do with a gun."

It was at that moment the report came. It sounded like the deafening blast of a high-caliber weapon.

All of them stood there a moment, staring at each other, and then Hamilton said, "That sounded like a gun."

"It came from the direction of the tennis courts," Norah said. "But I'm not going out to look."

Hamilton rose. "The switch is right here for the back yard. It could be that—" He went over to throw the switch as Joe went out the door he'd just entered.

The tennis courts were below and not in use. Between them and the clubhouse there was a steep slope and Joe was staring down into the darkness of this slope when the lights went on.

There was a man lying about halfway down, a tall, thin man. Joe hesitated only a second before going down that way. There was no other human being in sight.

Hamilton came out to stand on the sidewalk above. "Be careful, Joe. We don't know—" He broke off without finishing the sentence.

Joe took one look at the mutilated face beneath him. He could smell burned powder in the air, but it wasn't that that was turning his stomach.

He called to Hamilton, "Phone the police immediately. It's Bruce Dysart, and he's been shot right in the middle of the face. He's dead."

He stood there on the slope, looking all around, but there was no sign of human activity anywhere but on the playground, and they were all kids. And three hundred feet from this slope.

There was no gun in Dysart's hand; there was no gun in sight on the flood-lighted slope. There was a partial page from the *Los Angeles Times* lying about eight feet from the body but that had about as much significance as the banana peel a few feet from it, or the dead leaves littering the slope.

A little lower down a piece of bright yellow cardboard caught his eye and he went down to pick it up.

It was torn across the middle and there was a single word in black script on it. The word was *Smith*.

CHAPTER THREE

He stayed there near the body, keeping the curious kids back, until the law arrived.

He knew both of the detectives who came. They were out of the West Side Station, both sergeants. The brighter one of the duo was Sergeant Krivick, and he took Joe to one side, while the other man went down to wait for the ambulance.

Krivick said, "You live out here, or are you here officially?"

"I live out here. I left the Department some time ago, Ernie. I was in the clubhouse when we heard this shot. One of the men in the clubhouse turned on the lights while I went outside. And there he was. He's Bruce Dysart, a movie producer. Releases out of Paramount, I guess."

Krivick nodded. "A big, big man. Headline material, Joe. Anything you know about it?"

Joe took a breath. "Well—" He paused.

Krivick said softly, "Murder, Joe. I don't have to tell you about murder. No friends in this kind of case."

"All right. Dysart was supposed to come here, tonight, to meet a Miss Sharon Cassidy. She—or at least *he thought* she had leaked some information about a production of his. He was hot about it. She was telling us the story in the kitchen, there, when we heard the shot."

"She was admitting Dysart was hot at her?"

"That's right. Yesterday, I was at the beach with Dysart and this Sharon, and they quarreled about it then. And Dysart mentioned somebody else, a man with horn-rimmed glasses who must have passed the information on to Sharon. Dysart said he'd 'take care of him,' whatever he meant by that."

"I see. And Joe, what were you doing here?"

Joe studied Krivick a second before replying. "I joined this little theater group which meets here. There's a rehearsal tonight. That was some question, Ernie."

"Standard. You know that, Joe. Yesterday, you're with Dysart. Is that your kind of crowd? You a millionaire, Joe?"

"I guess. Just about. Didn't you hear about the inheritance?"

"No." In the dimness, Krivick studied him. "What's this—a gag?"

"Hell, no. Don't you guys get any news on the West Side? I inherited a wad from an aunt, quit the Force, and bought a home out here."

"I'll be damned." Krivick took out a pack of cigarettes, started to withdraw one, then paused and offered the pack to Joe. "Hey, I'd better be good to you. Millionaire. A dumb Irish dick a millionaire. Holy Christ!"

Joe laughed. "Sure. You get rough with me, I'll get the *Times* on your neck. You're talking to royalty now."

Krivick took a deep puff of his cigarette and brought his notebook up into the light coming through the kitchen windows. "Who was in the kitchen when you heard the shot?"

"Norah Payne, Walter Hamilton, Sharon Cassidy, and yours truly."

Krivick wrote them all down. "What do you know about them?"

"Norah's a realtor, Hamilton's in the investment business, Sharon Cassidy is an actress, and I'm just an ordinary big shot."

"And how about the rest of them? On the stage? In the auditorium? Or maybe out in the back, hunting?"

"I don't know, Ernie. I'd only been here a few minutes."

"And this guy with the horn-rimmed glasses—who is he?"

"I don't know. He isn't a member of the Players, I'm sure. That's the only way Dysart identified him yesterday."

Krivick was facing the kitchen windows and he said, "That wouldn't be the man, in there next to that redhead, now, near the stove?"

Joe turned to look into the lighted kitchen. A tall man, with a hooked, thin nose and black hair in a crew cut was standing next to Sharon Cassidy. They were talking very earnestly. The man wore horn-rimmed glasses.

"I never saw him before," Joe said. "It very well could be. That's Sharon Cassidy he's talking to."

"Uh-huh. Some woman, eh? Know her well, Joe?"

"No."

"You'd like to, I'll bet. Wait here." Krivick went to the doorway and through it, and Joe saw him gesture to the tall man.

Joe watched Sharon as the man left her side. Her body was held stiffly erect, and her eyes followed the pair all the way to Joe.

Here, Krivick said, "Could I have your name, please?"

"Alan Dysart."

A pause, and then Krivick said, "You are related to the —the deceased?"

"He was my uncle."

"Oh. I see. I'm sorry that I have to—"

"Don't be," Dysart said brusquely. "I can't think of anyone who meant less to me."

"Oh? You didn't get along?"

"Definitely not. We never have."

"I see. What did *you* do when you heard the shot?"

"I didn't hear it. I've just arrived."

"From home?"

"Well, not immediately from home. I spent some time in a bookstore in Santa Monica."

"Before that, you were home?"

"Yes."

"You live with your uncle?"

"Of course not. We saw as little of each other as possible."

"Mmmm-hmmm. What'd you do with the gun?"

"I have no gun. Officer, are you suggesting that I—"

Krivick waved a flat hand. "Of course not." He raised his voice to a uniformed officer who was standing near the kitchen door. "Come here, Deke."

As the officer started over, Krivick turned back to Dysart. "Why did you tell Sharon Cassidy about your uncle casting *Week End Widow?*"

"It was just a conversation we had. I didn't think it had any significance beyond proving to her how unscrupulous and completely commercial he was. It was just a symbol, you might say, of his piratical personality."

"You might say it," Krivick told him. "Not me." He turned to the uniformed officer. "Tell Adams I want a paraffin test on Mr. Dysart here, and scrapings from his shoes and both shoe prints. And then I want him held until I get back to the station."

Dysart stood there a second, staring at Krivick, and then the uniformed man touched his arm. "This way, Mr. Dysart."

Alan Dysart's laugh was short. "Dick Tracy. Oh, gawd—" He turned and went with the officer.

Krivick pulled out another cigarette. "Dick Tracy? I noticed his muddy shoes. That's more in the Sherlock Holmes line. Right, Joe?"

"You looked pretty good there for a while," Joe admitted. "I'd say maybe a Texas League Philip Marlowe."

"I hope he's guilty, anyway," Krivick said. "I hate these bright bastards."

Joe said nothing.

"*He* hated his uncle. I never heard anything bad about Bruce Dysart, and I been in this town a long, long time. Right, Joe?"

"Right. You've been in this town a long, long time. Going to give 'em all paraffin tests?"

"All but the four in the kitchen. I guess your word on them is good enough for me. How soon after the shot did you get outside?"

"I'd say ten or fifteen seconds. No more than that. And there wasn't anybody in sight but the kids on the playground. And they were a long ways off. And he was too low on the hill for anybody to nail him from the playground."

"I see. Guess I'll talk to that redhead. Want to go along?"

"Not unless you order it. I feel like Judas right now. These people are my friends."

"Thought you didn't know her well."

"Not well enough. But I know her. And the other girl who was in the kitchen about ten minutes ago is a real friend of mine."

"That would be the blonde?"

"Norah Payne, yes. A very fine girl. And the man is Walter Hamilton, a highly respected gent in these parts."

"My, my." Krivick shook his head. "You do travel in elite circles, Mr. Burke." He walked off toward the kitchen.

Then, from the shadows of the overhang near the office, Norah came over to stand next to Joe. "Isn't it horrible?"

"Yes. I've seen a lot of it. But I've never been involved this closely. It doesn't figure." He brought out a package of cigarettes and lighted one for her.

"Thanks." She looked up at him. "The bird with the

horn-rimmed glasses Dysart talked about—that would be Alan Dysart, wouldn't it?"

"I guess it would. Know anything about him?"

"Not much. Dabbled in experimental theater, worked as a writer at Columbia, tried painting." Her voice faltered. "God, I'm scared."

From the direction of the slope, a flash bulb went off.

Joe said, "Nobody's after you, honey. Calm down."

In the kitchen, a photographer and reporter were talking to Sergeant Krivick. Sharon still stood near the stove.

"Headline kill," Joe said. "This will make a seven-day wonder in all the papers. I told the sergeant about the beach yesterday, and what Sharon admitted tonight. He'll want to talk to you."

Then, from the direction of the slope, Joe saw the lads in white with their burden, and he took Norah's arm. "Let's go into the auditorium."

"I want the air," she protested, and then looked past him and must have seen the stretcher bearers. "All right."

Two uniformed officers were chasing the kids out of the auditorium, ordering them to go directly home. Along the far wall, the other members of the Players sat in a long row on folding chairs. *A Kiss for Kate* had a large cast.

At a table set under the basketball backboard, Krivick's partner was questioning Larry Puma. He finished with him and gestured toward the girl in the first chair along the wall.

Larry came back to where Joe and Norah were sitting. He looked worried.

Joe told him, "Routine questioning, Larry. You've nothing to fear unless you're guilty."

"And no reason to be guilty," Norah added. "What is it they look for, Joe? Isn't it motive, means, and opportunity?"

Joe nodded, studying the line of players along the wall.

Puma said, "This is the night I had to be late. This

night I couldn't be here and on the stage when Dysart dies. Typical Larry Puma timing. What's that business with the wax, Joe?"

"Are they doing that here?"

"In the property room. They did it to me and to Sharon and Walter Hamilton already."

"It's a way of searching for burned powder. An old gun will have some blow-by. Did you hear the shot, Larry?"

"I think so. It was about the time I turned off Sunset. I wouldn't hear it from that distance, though, would I?"

"I think so. Sam keep you working late tonight?"

"No. What is this? Are you back on the Force, or something?"

"No. I was thinking that if you were in hearing range of the shot, and coming up this way on Alma Real, you might have noticed somebody running away from this direction. He sure as hell got out of here in a hurry."

"That would be a breeze," Larry said. "I can get out of sight from that basin in ten seconds."

"How do you know? Did you ever try it?"

Larry looked over at Joe. "Sure. Practicing for the murder." He took a package of cigarettes from his pocket and lighted one. "Now that you have the opportunity established, how about the motive?"

Norah said lightly, "Well, you're such a fan of Sharon's, and Dysart was coming over here to talk to her and what he had to say wasn't going to be pleasant. So, naturally, out of your deep love for Sharon, you intercepted him and—" Norah stopped short and put a hand on Joe's knee. "Stop me; I'm getting hysterical."

Larry looked at her curiously. "Is that true—Dysart was coming over here to see Sharon?"

Joe nodded.

Larry shook his head. "Another idol fallen. I always thought he put out *good* pictures."

"He did," Norah said quietly. "As good as any profitable

picture can be. He wasn't coming here to talk contract, Larry. He had a bone to pick with Sharon."

"Okay. I can mourn him, then. There aren't many left with his integrity."

Joe said, "You and young Dysart don't agree. He thinks his uncle was a pirate, unscrupulous and completely commercial."

Larry nodded. "I know the kid. He knows less about more subjects than any other phony his age." Larry took a deep puff of his cigarette. "If I were a cop, he'd be my number one pick. The kid has no balance."

"He's no kid, really," Joe said. "He must be twenty-five."

"Some people are kids at eighty," Larry explained. "Including some of the cinema's finest 'arteests.' Emotional adolescents."

Joe stood up. "If Sharon and Hamilton had a paraffin test, I'd better have one, too. I'll be back."

In the kitchen, Krivick was finishing his questioning of Sharon, and Joe told him what he wanted.

Krivick shrugged. "I don't get it, Joe."

"I don't want you to play any favorites, Ernie. Hamilton and Sharon were in the kitchen with me. I'm just as suspect as they are."

"Okay. Testing them wasn't my idea; my partner got to it before I got a chance to talk to them. But if you insist, a man of your standing in the community—" He went over to open the door that led to the prop room. "Mr. Joe Burke next, Charley. He demands it."

From the next room, Charley Adams said, "It will be a pleasure. Maybe we can frame the plutocrat."

As they waited for Charley to finish the job he was on, Joe said, "Maybe you shouldn't have sent all those kids home, Ernie. Some of the kids these days—"

"Sure. But they were too far away, you said. And it **couldn't have been done from a distance; there's powder** burns. So—?"

"So they can run like hell, those kids, and—"

Krivick said quietly, "You want to handle it, Joe? I'll gladly step out."

"Sorry," Joe said. "You're right—I'm making like an indignant taxpayer."

From the next room, Charley called, "Okay. Send the big man in, Ernie."

When he went out again, there was a reporter talking to Larry and Norah. Joe was in time to hear the reporter ask, "This Dysart was a member of the Players?"

Larry shook his head. "No. He lived in the area, but he wasn't active in our group."

The reporter glanced at Joe, glanced away and then back, and his eyes grew thoughtful. "I've seen *you* somewhere."

"No kidding? I'm out of Central Homicide. Beat it."

"Cut it out. I know you now. Joe Burke, the millionaire cop. What's this, a hobby with you now, this murder?"

"They call me in on the tough ones," Joe said.

"I'll bet. Seriously, what's the story? It should make a great angle."

"I live out here," Joe said. "When I heard the sirens, I had to come. That's all there is. That's the gospel."

"All right," the reporter said. "I'll get it from Krivick, anyway. That man *loves* ink."

Norah said, "Are we supposed to hang around, Joe? I'm getting awfully jittery. I could use a drink."

"I'll ask Sergeant Krivick," Joe told her. "I could use a drink myself."

"And I," Larry Puma said. "Put in a word for me, too, Joe, *my friend.*"

Krivick said it was all right, and they left. Larry had his car, and lived in Santa Monica; he told them he'd meet them at the Melody Club.

It was a low-ceilinged place, a half block off Wilshire,

with a colored three-piece combo playing quietly to themselves in one corner.

It was peaceful, it was dim, and the rhythmic melody from the trio was soothing. They all ordered bourbon and water.

Larry said, "I hate to be callous, but we've lost another night of rehearsal. And Lord, how we need it."

Norah said, "Being callous on the cheerful side, it will sell out the house for all three nights, I'll bet."

"But with what kind of audience?" Joe asked.

Norah smiled. "The only kind we care about, a *paying* audience. We can cut the comps to nothing on this one."

Joe stirred uncomfortably in his chair. "Look, a man is dead. He died tonight."

They both stared at him gravely. Then Larry said, "That's right. You're right. All I know is two-bit theater and Sam's Shoe Salon. That's become my world."

Norah said to Joe, "You must have seen a lot of corpses."

"I never could get used to it, though. Actually, I was too much of a softie for Homicide."

Norah nodded. "I think you would be. My glass is empty."

They emptied some glasses. Not crowding it, not going over the edge. Norah and Larry talked theater and it made good listening for Joe. The combo talked melodically to themselves and to anyone who wanted to listen.

The horror of the body on the slope grew dimmer, the memory of the crowding kids and the glaring bulbs began to recede.

A little before midnight, Larry said, "Well, *I* work for a living. And Sam doesn't hold with tardy clerks." He left some money on the table. "See you at rehearsal Thursday."

They watched his big back disappear through the door, and then Norah looked at Joe. "I've had enough, too. Will you be able to drive all right?"

"Very well. Whisky never gets to me in less than quarts."

"Big, strong man." She rose. "Though I'm not drunk, by any standards, I feel sentimental."

He studied her. "Are you trying to tell me something?"

"I'm not sure. Maybe the night air will make me sane again."

They went out and the night was warm, the wind still coming from the desert. Norah said, "We haven't had a winter like this since 1939."

"When you were four years old?"

"When I was sixteen. Now you know *that* about me. I should be old enough to know my mind, shouldn't I?"

"Don't make an issue of it. I haven't suggested a thing."

"No. But if it were Sharon, walking here with you— Oh, I'm talking nonsense."

He opened the door on the curb side for her. "I like the sound of it. You are the first woman I've met who seduced herself."

"I haven't. I've known you forty-eight hours, Joe Burke, and I'm *not* a tramp. I have gone through a horrible emotional experience tonight, and then the whisky—" She paused, as he walked around to open the other door and climb in behind the wheel.

She stared through the windshield. "Take me home, quickly."

"Yes, m'am." He kicked the hundred and eighty horses into life. "Isn't it a beautiful night? From my living-room, I can see all the coast lights, way down to Palos Verdes. And there'll be a moon, over the water. And you can hear the waves—"

"Shut up."

He cut down to the Coast Highway, and they could see the path of the full moon on the water. Joe asked, "Want a cigarette?"

"No, thank you."

"I'm getting to like that Larry Puma. He's no dummy about show business, is he?"

"Larry is very discerning and knowledgable about the theater."

Joe laughed. "Duchess, who are you fighting?"

"It's 'whom.'"

"Who's hoom?"

Silence, and then she laughed faintly. "You bum. You Irish bum."

"Want a cigarette?"

"All right. Friends, aren't we, Joe? Always friends?"

"Always. And don't be anything you don't want to be with me. And be anything you do want to be. I'm not a complete slob, you know."

"I know." She'd lighted a cigarette, and he could feel her eyes on him. "And you are handsome. And clean, no doubt. And gentle?"

"Don't talk it to death. When I get to the stop light on Via, you can say 'turn left,' if you want. That's the way I live, to the left. Otherwise, I drive straight on and deposit you safely at your apartment. But don't yak about it; that's too phony for me."

"All right, Joe. Lordy, what a beautiful night."

He nodded. They'd stopped for the light at Chautauqua, and when it changed, he turned right, climbing toward Sunset. He wondered if she was thinking about Dick Metzger, who'd driven his Jaguar off this cliff three years ago.

At the bend of Sunset, they stopped for the sign, and she said, "Alan Dysart is the one that sergeant suspects, isn't he?"

"I don't know. The sergeant doesn't like him."

"So, could he railroad him?"

"No."

"Is this just loyalty to the Force, Joe?"

"No. Sergeant Krivick's a pretty good man. Even if he

wanted to frame somebody, it would be impossible, after the murder. And that isn't done, despite what you read in the newspapers."

She sighed. "I have kind of a soft spot for the Alan Dysart type, young men in revolt. Haven't you?"

"No. I've jailed too many of them."

Talk, above the pound of his heart. The car moved steadily, though his hands on the wheel trembled. She talked, but the words had no meaning to him.

They passed the theater and the shopping district and the light on Via was flashing in a steady caution warning. The light grew bigger and Norah grew quiet.

Then, just as the front wheels entered the intersection, she said, "Turn left, Joe."

Not another word from either of them all the way to his house. There, as he closed the front door behind them, she said, "No lights. I can see the place in the morning."

And a little later: "Be gentle with me, honey. It's been three years."

In the morning, when he wakened, he was alone in the room and he wondered if she'd left during the night. A remarkable girl. For a moment he thought of the dilettante who'd gone over the cliff, and the thought pained him.

She was too nice a girl for playboys. And too nice for a plaything. He remembered Walter Hamilton's, "She's a really fine girl—" Well, damn it, he hadn't pressured her. He was glad it had happened, but he hadn't laid any plans for it. And now she was gone.

He thought—until he smelled the coffee. And heard the closing of the refrigerator door. He rose and put on a robe and went out to the kitchen.

Her back was to him; she was plugging the toaster into the breakfast-nook receptacle.

"Good morning," he said.

She turned and there was the faintest color in her cheeks. "Good morning, beast."

"You're blushing."

"I don't do this every day. Or night. Aren't you going to shave?"

"I'm going to shave. I just wanted to look at you, first. I thought you'd gone and it—disturbed me."

She smiled. "Thank you. It was only a crumb, but it helps. Do you like me, Joe?"

"I like you, Norah Payne. I will go to make myself pretty for you." He winked at her, and went out.

As he shaved, he smiled. And shaving, he naturally saw the smile. And seeing it, he stopped smiling. It had looked too much like a smirk. He was no smirker.

Beeg man, he told himself. *Beeg, lustful, dominating animal, you dumb Irish bastard. You're just lucky.*

Adultery wasn't a game he could completely enjoy. He had left the church at twenty-one, but he still remembered all the things Father Riley had told him.

Orange juice and scrambled eggs and little pork sausages. Toast and marmalade and coffee. Everything just right.

Even the pompous *Times* had given the death of Bruce Dysart a big splash on the first page. For Dysart had not only been a famous man; he had been a wealthy one and politically active in the industry on the *Times's* side of the fence.

The words *heinous, barbarous, fiendish* and *brutal* were used. No lead as to the identity of the killer was stated, though the holding of Alan Dysart was given enough ink. And the *Times* made it clear *he* was no Republican.

Norah said, "They don't know any more now than they did last night, do they?"

"The newspapers don't. But the police might. They're holding young Dysart."

"They would."

"Was he a—or is he a Commie?"

"I don't know. He was in college when Wallace ran, and I read he was making speeches for Wallace around the campus. He went to UCLA."

"That was kind of a hot bed, at one time, wasn't it?"

"UCLA? No. If you want to go to a major college in this town, and you don't play football, where else can you go?"

"Loyola. He was probably one of those parlor pinks."

Norah took a deep breath. "Joe, you're not *real* right wing, are you?"

"I voted·for Ike. Krivick is going to give that kid a workout; you can be sure. The kid's too lippy."

"Around policemen I have a tendency to become lippy myself. They bring out the worst in me."

He grinned at her. "I know it."

She was reaching for a cup to throw when the front door chime sounded. She paused to stare at Joe, her hand still reaching for the cup.

"Migawd," she said hoarsely. "Who could it be?"

"Somebody selling vacuum cleaners."

"Not this time of the morning. Don't go."

Joe leaned back in his chair to where he could see through the dining-room wing to the front porch. "It's Sharon Cassidy."

Norah's chin went up and she lifted a hand to fluff out her hair. "Open the door, Joe. Bring her in for a cup of coffee. *This,* I want her to see."

CHAPTER FOUR

At the door, Sharon said, "I have to see you, Joe. Alan needs your help."

"My help? Come in. Have you had breakfast?"

"I could certainly use a cup of coffee. That poor kid is being— Oh, it's a mess."

They came into the kitchen.

Sharon paused, staring at Norah. "Oh? Hello, Norah."

"Hello, dear. I just dropped in for a cup of coffee."

"I'll bet. Last night." Sharon sat across from her.

Joe sat down on the bench next to her. "You called him a kid. He's more than that, Sharon. Larry called him that, too. The Department's more realistic. They consider a twenty-five-year-old male a man. He should start acting like one."

"They're trying to railroad him," Sharon said. "I got him a lawyer, but I thought you, having been a policeman and all, might be able—"

Joe said, "I can find out what the real story is on him. But I certainly can't interfere in the Department's business." He poured her a cup of coffee. "You two aren't—I mean he isn't—" He held both hands out, palms up. "What do I want to say?"

"You want to know if she's soft on him," Norah said. "Are you, Sharon?"

"Of course not. I admire him, tremendously, but, well, he's so—so immature."

"He's probably the only heir," Norah said acidly, "though I'm sure Bruce Dysart wouldn't mention him if he left a will."

Sharon said, "That wasn't necessary, Norah."

Norah nodded gravely. "I apologize. It wasn't." She looked at Joe, and away.

Sharon said, "What about that paraffin test they took? Wouldn't that clear him?"

Joe shook his head. "It would depend on the gun. They don't know what kind of gun was used yet, probably. I'll tell you what I'll do, Sharon. I'll get in touch with Sergeant Krivick today, and then I'll phone you. You're in the West Los Angeles book, are you?"

"No. It's an unlisted number."

Joe found a piece of paper and a pencil and wrote it down. Then he asked, "Couldn't I fix you something to eat? You look beat out, lassie."

"I couldn't eat anything. That Sergeant Krivick goes out of his way to be rude, doesn't he?"

"He's rough," Joe admitted. "But he's a good officer. He wouldn't try to railroad anyone, Sharon. We have a fine Police Department in Los Angeles. I mean that."

Norah slid out and stood up. "Well, I have to get back to the office. Thanks for the coffee, Joe."

"Wait for me," Sharon said. "I'll drive you over. Unless your car is somewhere around? I didn't see it."

"I'll wait," Norah said. She went through the doorway that led to the dining-room.

Sharon sipped her coffee and rummaged in her purse for a cigarette. "That girl certainly doesn't like me, does she?"

"I imagine most women don't." He held a light for her.

"You're right about that," she said, and blew smoke past him. "And I don't give a damn. Women bore me silly."

Joe chuckled. "Not me. I've always found them good company."

She nodded. "I'll accept that. Some place you have here."

"It's kind of cozy." He lighted a cigarette for himself. "Have you known Alan very long?"

"Two years. He was directing at an experimental theater in Redondo Beach. It folded, of course; those things need a genius. But I was impressed with his—oh, fire, I suppose is the easy word for it. Actually, he's a very interesting lad. But romantically—?" She shrugged. "Well, you've seen him."

"He didn't look too repulsive to me."

"I didn't mean physically. But he looks so—young."

"And he's brought out the maternal in you?"

"That's nicer than what Norah said." She stood up and stretched. "I'm dead."

The stretch had brought her chief allure into prominence. Joe pretended not to notice.

Then Norah came out into the kitchen. "It's a nice house, Joe." She was carrying her purse and the short coat she'd worn last night. She looked at Sharon. "Ready to go?"

"Ready." She looked at the coat, and smiled.

Norah flushed, but said nothing.

Joe said, "Drop in any time, girls. I never run out of coffee."

Sharon nodded. "Don't forget about phoning that sergeant."

He went to the door with them and watched them drive off. Sharon's car, he saw, was a replica of the '47 Chev he'd traded in.

He did the dishes and went into the bedroom to make the bed. The scent of Norah's fragrance was still in there. He was hanging up his clothes, checking the pockets as he did, when he came across the piece of cardboard he'd picked up on the slope last night.

He told Krivick about it when he finally got him on

the phone.

"What kind of cardboard?" Krivick asked. "You mean —you think it's important or something?"

"I'm not getting paid to think, Ernie. It's a piece of yellow cardboard with the word *Smith* on it and I found it on the slope."

"Near the body? On the body?"

"No. Twenty feet away. I just thought I'd mention it. How about Alan Dysart?"

"He went home fifteen minutes ago. I haven't got a case, but I'd like to fit one around him. Looks like he's the heir; that should be motive enough, huh?"

"Not for a purely artistic young man."

"Cut out the crap. I've been in this business a long time, and I never met an artist yet that hated money. They just hate somebody else having it."

"Yes, Captain. Are you coming out this way today?"

"In about an hour. You'll be home?"

"I'll be home." Joe gave him the address and hung up.

The ridiculous Chamber of Commerce weather had persisted; it was another beautiful day. Joe took the books on little theater he'd checked out yesterday and went into the study.

But he couldn't get interested. He put some Chopin on the record player and stretched out on a green leather couch. He was half asleep when Sergeant Krivick rang his bell.

The sergeant stood in the middle of the huge living-room and shook his head. "You really hit the jackpot, didn't you?"

"Yup. Have you any favorites in this case besides Alan Dysart?"

He shrugged. "I haven't *any* favorites, Joe. Where's that piece of cardboard?"

Joe went into the bedroom to get it. When he came back, Krivick was in the kitchen, admiring all the tile. He looked at the cardboard casually, turning it over in his hand.

"What makes you think it could be important?"

"I don't, necessarily. But it looked clean and new compared to the other rubbish around there. And I suppose it caught my eye, being bright yellow."

"Mmmmm. Smith—it wouldn't be a calling card, yellow like this."

"No. It's not the right stock for a calling card, either."

"There's a Leonard Smith in that gang of actors, but he's one of the best alibied in the bunch. I'll have this checked." Krivick put the piece of cardboard in his pocket. "What do you know about that gang?"

"Not much. I just joined them a couple days ago. They're all amateurs though about half of them have had some professional experience. Young Dysart directed at an experimental theater in Redondo Beach. Larry Puma has directed and acted in a dozen amateur groups around town."

"That's the guy who was late for rehearsal, that Puma, wasn't it?"

"He said he was. I didn't see him come in. I was in the kitchen. He's directing the current play. Did you get the slug?"

"No. It went right through his head. I've a couple men combing the park, right now."

"It entered through the face, though, didn't it?"

"Right."

"And he was lying on his back," Joe went on. "That should mean he was facing downhill. He wouldn't be, if he was just walking up the slope from his house."

"I don't follow you, Joe."

"If he was walking toward the killer, uphill, he'd fall forward, wouldn't he? Isn't the body always balanced *against* the slope, walking up or down?"

"Sure. But aren't you forgetting the impact of a slug

in the face."

"No. The impact would stop him, coming up, but if he was influenced by that, he'd fall either flat forward on his face, or he'd spin and fall with his head pointing down the slope. He was on his back, his head higher than his feet. He'd have to turn. Somebody must have stopped him, coming up the slope, and he turned to see who it was or talk to him, and—bingo."

Krivick was frowning. "That adds, Joe. You're right. That would put the killer below him on the slope. In about twenty steps from the bottom of the slope, the killer could get to that service yard, there. You know, he could have been hiding behind that big incinerator, waiting for you to turn your back to him. When you did, he took off through the yard and up to Toyopa."

Joe nodded. "I asked Larry Puma last night if he'd seen anybody running up that way. Larry heard the shot."

They were walking through the house as they talked, and they were now in Joe's bedroom.

Krivick sniffed and looked wonderingly at Joe.

"Kind of sissy for shaving lotion, isn't it?" Joe admitted. "The girls seem to like it, though."

"My wife does," Krivick said. "That's the scent she wears. I'm glad she was at my mother's house, last night."

Joe shrugged. "You know how it is, when you're handsome and rich."

"Not me, not either one. Well, Joe, keep your ears and eyes open for me, won't you? Once a cop, always a cop. Right, Joe?"

"Right, Ernie. Say hello to the west side gang for me."

"Sure will. We'll have to come out here for poker some night."

"I've got the cards and the chips," Joe said, "and they've never been used."

Since Dysart had been released, Joe didn't phone Sharon as he'd promised. Because there was no point in telling her Krivick didn't have a case against Alan; she would undoubtedly forward the information to Alan. And it wasn't a thing Krivick would want repeated.

At noon, he went to the center to eat, and then over to the park. The playground was loaded with kids from the parochial school near by; the tennis courts were in use. He stood on the top of the slope behind the kitchen, studying the road that led to the service yard.

The only place of concealment was the incinerator, as Krivick had suggested. He went over to stand behind that.

There was no place to run from here, except back toward the clubhouse. It was surrounded by a high cyclone fence. And the gate would undoubtedly be locked at night.

Of course, over under the trees, there was that barbecue grill and oven, but that would require a long flight through a lighted area.

Joe came around the end of the building to study the curved drive that ran in front of the main door. And here he saw the best possibility for escape. There was a parking area here.

If the killer had any guts, he wouldn't run away from the clubhouse. He'd run *up* the slope, past the body, to this area and get into his car.

The corner of the building would shield him from Joe's vision. Then, as the hubbub grew, he could step out of his car, as though he'd just arrived, and walk leisurely to the front door.

He? Why did he think of the killer as a "he"? It could just as well be a "she." Either way, this was the logical escape route. The killer could expect a certain amount of indecision from the people in the clubhouse and even the possibility that no one would come out to investigate the noise.

No, he couldn't expect that with a playground full of

kids. Or *she* couldn't. Kids are too nosy.

Joe turned back toward the clubhouse and saw a man watching him. Joe had seen him around the clubhouse on rehearsal night but didn't know his name. He was a dark, stocky man.

Joe smiled, as the man came over, and said, "How are you?"

"Worried," the man said. "I've suddenly been given special attention by the police. Aren't you Joe Burke, the—former policeman?"

"That's right. I'm not sure we've met."

"We haven't. My name is Leonard Smith. Have you any—I mean, could you guess why I am suddenly singled out for special consideration?"

"I've no idea," Joe lied. "The Department overlooks nothing, of course."

"Everything was routine, until about half an hour ago," Smith went on. "I received no more attention than the rest of the players. And then, this noon, Sergeant Krivick picked me up at the house and brought me over here. He said he wanted some information, that he needed help from someone familiar with the area and I seemed to be one of the few members who was home during the day."

"That makes sense," Joe said.

"Perhaps. But once here, his questioning led me to believe I was more than a guide. I hardly knew Dysart; I'd certainly have no reason to—to, well, do what was done to him."

"How did you happen to know him?" Joe asked. "Was he ever active in the Players?"

"No. He produced the first picture I ever worked on. I was an assistant dialogue director on *Galagan Ridge.*"

"That was a great picture," Joe said. "I saw it twice, and I'm no movie fan."

"He was a great producer," Smith said. "He had enough taste to avoid the banal and enough sense to avoid the arty. I could use a drink, couldn't you?"

"The afternoon is yawning at me," Joe agreed, "but there aren't any bars in this neck of the woods."

"There's one less than three blocks from here," Smith said. "Mine."

Joe put a hand on the stocky man's shoulder. "What are we standing around for? Let's go."

As they climbed into Joe's new car, Smith asked, "Is this standard transportation for retired detectives?"

"No. I inherited some money."

"Oh? You wouldn't be interested in backing a picture, would you? A low budget, extremely fine picture with great commercial possibilities?"

"Not this afternoon," Joe said.

"Of course. We'll talk about it another time. I had to ask, though."

Leonard Smith's home was small but not cheap, with a view of the sea. The walls were shingled, the roof was a shake roof, and the small front yard was buried in shrubs and flowers.

As they went up the flagstone walk to the front door, Smith said, "I could sell it, this minute, at a ten-thousand-dollar profit. I bought it before prices went crazy out here."

The living-room was cozy French provincial and a little too dainty for Joe's taste. The study was better, paneled in etched plywood.

The bookshelves that flanked the fireplace were shoulder high and crammed with books, all the books Joe hadn't understood and hundred of others. The walls above the bookshelves were almost solid with autographed portraits of studio personalities.

One portrait stood alone on the low mantel, an excellent photographic study of Sharon Cassidy. It was inscribed: *With all my love.*

Joe stared at it for some seconds.

"Beautiful girl," Smith said.

Joe nodded.

"And completely without scruples," Smith added. "Though, with my experience, I certainly should have been wary of the type." He went to the small leatherette bar in one corner of the room. "What will it be, Joe?"

"Bourbon and water, please. Sharon give you a bad time?"

"Not bad. I made the mistake of thinking she was interested in me."

"And she wasn't?"

Smith chuckled. "Take another look at me, Joe. Short and plain and stout. Imagine yourself in Sharon's shoes. Would you be?"

"Looks aren't everything, if you'll pardon the frankness."

"No. There's influence and money, too. I didn't have quite enough of either. But I don't regret it. Norah Payne is the kind of girl I'd like to settle down with. It's only that I feel so silly with taller women."

"She's a great girl," Joe agreed. He took the drink Smith was handing him. "You've retired, too, Mr. Smith?"

"More or less. Though not of my own volition. Only two kinds of people are employed in the industry right now, the extremely competent and the superlative schemers. I'm neither." He went over to sit in a huge leather chair.

"Television, I suppose," Joe said. "How about this new three-dimensional stuff?"

"Your guess is as good as mine. Maybe, if they'd had *three-dimensional characters* from the start, this TV garbage would be no threat." He chuckled. "The movies could be the first major entertainment medium destroyed by wrestlers."

"Major or minor," Joe corrected him.

"Well, no. Wrestling was destroyed by wrestlers."

"I'll have another drink on that one," Joe said.

Smith nodded and rose. "And I."

He brought a pair back from the bar with him, and Joe asked, "Did you know Dick Metzger?"

"Slightly." Smith paused a moment before handing Joe his drink. "What made you think of Dick Metzger?"

"Well, you mentioned Norah Payne before, and I suppose I've been thinking of her, more or less, since. And thinking of Norah made me think of this Metzger."

"You didn't know him, then?" Smith went back to his chair.

"No. I never heard of him until Sharon mentioned him, the other night, and I saw the reaction it got from Norah."

"He wasn't much," Smith said. "A tall and wealthy bundle of charm. In a way he could be called a namedropper. Only the names he dropped were Plato and Spinoza, Hindemith and Brahms, Rembrandt and Picasso and dozens of others, equally renowned. He knew nothing of these gentlemen beyond the names, but the circles he moved in weren't likely to discover that. A thirty-two carat fraud."

"You didn't like him, I take it?"

Smith frowned. "What the hell is this, Joe, an investigation?"

"Yes. But not of you. I'm interested in the kind of man who'd interest Norah Payne."

Smith studied Joe a moment. "Why? You don't think Norah had anything to do with his death, do you?"

"That wasn't why I asked. Let's talk about the Rams."

They talked about the Rams and the unusual weather, about the Players and the Police Department and the Palisades and the murder. Whisky went with the talk, and Joe relaxed on the chaise longue near the fireplace where he could watch the sea.

It must have been strong whisky. For the talk grew dimmer in his ears, and he dozed off.

When he wakened, it was growing dark outside. Leonard Smith was still sitting in the big leather chair, but he was now asleep.

Joe rose to study the pictures on the wall. There were some big names here, and all of the pictures were autographed with affection. He went over to stand in front of Sharon's picture.

"Attention-compelling, isn't she?" came from behind him.

Joe turned to find Smith's eyes on him. "She even dominates this gang. Only—sex, isn't it?"

"Only? It's a rather important force. It's an attraction that reaches men at all intellectual levels. And all social levels. Sharon used her power crudely, or she'd be under contract today, and not at a hundred a week."

"How was that?"

"I'm not a tale bearer. There's a Board of Directors' meeting at eight. Are you going?"

"I'm not a member of the Board."

"I am, and there's nothing secret about us. You may as well sit in. I've some steaks in the refrigerator. How about it?"

"You're too good to me," Joe said. "I'll fry the potatoes."

Norah was at the Board meeting and Walter Hamilton and Larry Puma and some others Joe knew only by sight. The treasurer, Pete Delahunt, gave the breakdown on the last production, which had been *Skylark*.

The total receipts at the door amounted to slightly over two hundred and thirty-four dollars. Total production costs had amounted to a bit over two hundred and thirty-eight dollars. However, there had been a profit of almost thirty dollars on the refreshments: doughnuts, lemonade, and coffee.

"Which," Pete finished, "gives us a total profit of twenty-five dollars and eighty cents, a highly profitable three-day showing."

Joe laughed—and looked up to discover he was the only one laughing. They were all looking at him painfully.

"I'm sorry," he said.

Pete Delahunt smiled. "And if Mr. Burke would like to pay his two dollars for a year's membership fee, we can add that to the kitty. And he can laugh all he wants."

"I'll pay," Joe said. "I was only thinking of Walter's dream of a building of our own. With one production a month, that gives us twenty-six dollars a month. I never saw anything at that price, out here."

Walter Hamilton nodded. "That's what keeps it a dream. But who wants attainable dreams?"

"I, for one," Norah said.

Larry Puma said, "Maybe we'll find an angel some day."

Hamilton told about the possibility of getting risers. If the Players would furnish the carpenter work, the Park Board would furnish the lumber.

"And we need risers," Walter pointed out. "Some of our steadiest customers have complained about getting stiff necks. Any volunteer carpenter in the room?"

Joe raised his hand, as did Smith and two others. Smith said, "Though I won't guarantee the quality of my work. And where will we store them when they're not being used? Not in that closet-sized prop room."

Hamilton shrugged. "We'll think of something." He leafed through some papers in front of him. "I have a letter here from Jed Bishop, a director at Paramount. It's in answer to a letter of mine asking him if he'd like to direct another of our productions. He would, and he'd like it to be *The Man Who Came to Dinner*. Any comment?"

Pete Delahunt said, "It hasn't been played around here for years. And everybody knows of it. It makes sense to me. How much of a cast would it take?"

"Thirty-six, unless we cut it."

Larry Puma said, "That nympho character in it would be a natural for Sharon."

"If anyone is taking notes, as she should be," Norah said, "I move that remark of Larry's be stricken from the record."

Larry shrugged. "I was speaking objectively. Miss Cassidy is your friend, Miss Payne?"

"They're *bosom* companions," Leonard Smith said, and ducked the purse Norah threw at him.

Hamilton rapped on the table for order. "All right, that's enough. And while we're on the subject of Sharon, I'd like to remind you she's one of *ours*. I've already heard in town about Dysart coming over to see her; that must have been leaked from our group. I've seen a lot of little theaters go to pot, and one of the main causes is a group breaking up into cliques. I don't want that to happen here. Sharon may not be your idea of the all-American girl, but she's one of us and she brings a lot of patrons through our door. If you can't get along with her, stay away from her."

There was a silence in the room, and everyone looked uncomfortable.

Leonard Smith said quietly, "That was a long speech for you, Walter. I'll second it."

Norah said humbly, "All right." Then: *"All right!"*

Hamilton said, "We're agreed, then, on *The Man Who Came to Dinner?*"

There was a chorus of "ayes."

"Opposed?"

Silence.

"And one more bit of good news," Walter went on. "The local Methodist Church is buying up the Thursday nights for the next four months at a hundred and ten dollars a night. That's four hundred and forty dollars we can pick up any time we want to."

Applause, murmurs, subdued jubilation.

Norah asked, "Will they want the kitchen, too?"

Hamilton nodded. "Inasmuch as we've averaged about thirty-five dollars a night for the last three Thursday nights, I thought it only fair for them to have the kitchen profit. They'll run it."

"And I can finally see a play," Norah said.

Which ended the Board's business. Larry and Walter and Smith went out to the stage for rehearsal. Norah and Joe went into the kitchen.

"You weren't home today," she told him. "I phoned."

"Why? Something I needed to know?"

She shook her head. "I just phoned. The beach, I suppose?"

He smiled, and shook his head.

"Riding around in that big car, I'll bet."

He shook his head.

"Golf?"

"I don't play it."

Silence. She went over to get one of the huge coffeepots. She brought it to the sink and half filled it. Joe came over to take it from her, and put it on the stove.

He offered her a cigarette, and she took it. She put it in her mouth, and he held a light for her. She didn't meet his gaze.

He put a finger under her chin and lifted her head up to where she was looking at him. "I was with Leonard Smith, all afternoon."

Her eyes were cool. "It's none of my business."

"Come on. I was teasing you before. Smith thought the police were suspecting him, and we got to talking about it, and then we went over to his house and had a few drinks and we both fell asleep. And then we made dinner, and came over here."

"Cozy, aren't you two?"

"He's a nice guy."

"All right. Did he come over to your house to tell you he was worried about the police?"

"No. We met here. I was looking over the scene of the crime, as they say in the magazines, and the police had brought him here. We recognized each other, and—well, that's it."

The door behind them opened, and Joe turned to see Sharon standing there.

She smiled. "I hope I'm not interrupting anything?"

Norah opened her mouth and closed it.

Joe said, "Your boy was released, wasn't he? You know about it, of course."

"I know about it, but he's not my boy. I thought you were going to phone me."

"By the time I got to Sergeant Krivick, Alan had already been released. So there wasn't any point in my phoning."

Sharon sighed. "You're a painfully honest man. Is there any coffee? I'm not on for ten minutes."

"There's some instant coffee in the prop room," Norah said. "I've just started the big pot."

Sharon went through to the prop room.

Norah asked, "And what did you learn, Ellery, after your investigation of the scene of the crime?"

"I saw a way it could be done." He told her his theory about the parking area.

"I see. And Leonard came late?"

"No. They investigated him for a different reason."

"A reason you are not prepared to divulge, Mr. Burke?"

"Exactly. No offense, now. I was a cop too long to go blabbing everything I know. Quit making like a wife."

"Yes," she said. "I see. Yes."

Sharon came back into the kitchen, a cup of coffee in her hand. "Fighting?"

Norah didn't answer. Joe started to answer, but then the door from the auditorium opened and Alan Dysart came in.

He looked pale and frightened. He said, "Sharon, I have to talk to you right away." He looked at Norah and Joe and then back at Sharon. "Alone."

CHAPTER FIVE

THEY WENT OUT TO THE PATIO, and Norah and Joe were again alone. Norah started to open a can of coffee, and Joe came over to take it from her.

He said, "You're grumpy tonight."

"I guess. Acting like a despoiled virgin, or something. Golly, didn't Alan look terrible?"

"Mmmm-hmmm. Hasn't he a mother to run to?"

"She lives in Italy. With her fifth husband. And his father is dead. I'm surprised Alan's as stable as he is. It's a damned shame, I think."

"You kind of like him, don't you?"

"Yes." Norah looked out the window toward where Alan and Sharon were talking. Then she looked back at Joe. "Jealous, flatfoot?"

"About Alan? No. It's the maternal in you." He set the opened coffee can on the big table. "Let's go and watch them rehearse."

In front of the stage, Larry Puma was saying, "Jed, when you beat your fist into your hand like that, keep both hands above the waist. Any gesture below waist level is inclined to be awkward. We'll try it again from Dorothy's entrance."

Twice more he stopped them after that, and then it began to come alive, to flow.

Norah whispered, "That water must be boiling by now. And just when this thing was starting to move."

"I'll get it," Joe said, and put a hand on her shoulder

to keep her from rising.

In the kitchen, Sharon sat alone at the big table.

"Alan gone?" Joe asked.

She nodded. "I told him to go home and get some sleep. He's worn out. Am I due on yet?"

"I think it's pretty close. They're in that part where Jed and Dorothy discover they have a mutual friend."

"Migawd, that's it." She rose quickly and went out toward the prop room.

Joe put twenty measures of coffee into the bubbling pot and checked his watch.

He came out into the auditorium again just in time to see Sharon make her entrance.

Leonard Smith was on the stage as a butler, his back to Sharon. She crossed to stage right and gazed out a nonexistent window toward a nonexistent patio.

Then she turned and said, "Arthur, you've arranged the patio very cleverly, and—"

"Just a second," Larry Puma said, and glanced at the script the stage manager was holding. "Didn't we change that? Wasn't Sharon supposed to say 'good evening' to the butler when she entered?"

"I should," Sharon said. "It's awkward, otherwise, though it isn't in the script." She smiled. "I was afraid, if I did, you might think I was trying to pad the part."

Norah whispered, "Here we go, again."

But Larry laughed. "My mistake. I never changed it. Come in again."

She made her entrance again and Larry didn't interrupt for a full five minutes.

"It's playing, now," Norah whispered. "That Puma man has done a fine job here."

Joe was no critic, nor reasonably accurate facsimile, but he could see what Norah meant. Larry's polishing had made them shine; the illusion was solid and communicative.

Joe whispered, "It's a damned crime, a guy with his moxie selling shoes."

"He's young," Norah said. "This is a slow business when you come up the right way."

How far "up" was this? Joe said nothing, thinking of Walter Hamilton and Leonard Smith, fairly wealthy men who didn't need the theater for a living, though they needed the theater. And he remembered the stories he'd read of how this or that now famous movie star had been discovered. One behind a soda fountain, another running an elevator. With no previous theatrical experience, as the columnists loved to mention.

Was it to be considered a virtue, not knowing your trade? Of the gang now on the stage, Sharon was undoubtedly the crudest. And yet she projected a lure that Hollywood could sell. Of the gang on the stage, or in this organization, Sharon would be the best Hollywood bet.

But who could blame the studios for that? They didn't make the public taste; they were businessmen and doomed to follow it. There were many great talents in the studios; John Wayne still remained the number-one box office draw.

"A penny for your thoughts," Norah whispered.

"We'd better go out and check that coffee."

In the kitchen, he turned the gas off under the coffee and brought out some cups from the cabinet.

"A penny for your thoughts, I repeat," Norah said.

"I was thinking of how hard those kids work, and for what? Actors with less ability are getting paid for it, aren't they?"

"I suppose. In any trade or art or craft or profession, breaks help, you know. Timing and single-mindedness are important, too."

"I don't understand all of that. Aren't they single-minded?"

"Not enough to put their whole attention to the job of

getting ahead, playing the angles, living for the break. Except Sharon, of course. She has one interest in life: the theatrical advance of Sharon Cassidy. And she'll do it, too, selling just as much of herself as she needs to at each step."

"You sound like a soap opera."

"She's right out of one, so typical it hurts. Haven't we another topic of conversation?"

"Well, last night—"

"Don't be vulgar."

"Last night," he went on, "when Larry was talking about plays and actors and playwrights, it all made sense, even to a moron like me. If he can get through to me, he can get through to any audience. It seems a crime that he's not able to land in TV, at least."

"He will. Joe, when Larry goes up, he'll *stay* up. His knowledge will be so wide and so sound that he'll be secure. He'll never get ulcers, not from fear, anyway."

"*If* he goes up."

Norah took a deep breath. "I could use a cup of that coffee. Did you and Mr. Smith come to any conclusions on the murder?"

Joe poured two cups of coffee and brought one to Norah. "Nope. He likes you. If you weren't too tall for him, he'd like to lead you to the altar."

"You discussed me?"

"He did. That's all he said. We were talking about Dick Metzger, too. Want a cigarette?"

"No, thank you. How did it happen you were talking about Dick Metzger?"

"I don't remember." Joe lighted a cigarette and sipped his coffee.

Norah glared at him. "Locker room talk, Joe, about me?"

"That's a rotten remark, lady. What the hell's the matter with you tonight?"

"Nothing a man could understand. All right, I'll take a cigarette."

He lighted it for her and she smiled at him. "Sensitive. I keep remembering it was *my* idea, last night. I feel like a tramp."

"Everybody knows you're a lady," Joe told her. "That's one thing we all agree on. And it wasn't only *your* idea, last night. And you're a big girl now; act like one."

"All right. Kiss me."

He came around to her end of the table and kissed her.

And from the doorway, someone said, "How romantic!"

It was Sharon, and the others were behind her. Joe grinned and went to pour the coffee as Norah turned beet-red.

They settled around the big table. Larry Puma had taken the chair on one side of Norah, Smith the other, by the time Joe had finished pouring the coffee.

There was an empty chair next to Sharon, and Joe took it. Sharon said softly, "You're going to be in trouble. Norah won't like this."

"We're not married," he said.

"Yet."

From the other end of the table, Joe caught Norah watching them. As his eyes met hers, she looked away.

Sharon said, "Norah can get awfully intense about a man."

"Like Dick Metzger?"

"That was the last one. I wouldn't say you were in the same pattern." She paused. "Except you're wealthy, too."

"Meee-iouw," Joe said. The scent Sharon wore must have been heavy with musk. Joe felt the pulse beating in his wrists.

She made a production out of lighting a cigarette.

Joe said, "If you'll permit me a layman's opinion, I think you're wrong on Larry Puma. He's certainly shaping this show into something."

"Oh, I suppose he's really competent enough. Larry hasn't any—push, any fire. That's his big lack."

"Any brass, you mean. I like him."

She smiled. "It's a free country. He doesn't like me, so I return the favor. I'm not a really popular girl in this gang." She blew a big cloud of smoke. "But I'm not crying about it. I'm not pathological enough to need friends like some people do. I enjoy my own company."

Joe said, "But you seemed very concerned about Alan Dysart. He's special, huh?"

"He will be, in a week or so. He'll be rich."

"You mean that his uncle left him the estate? Alan's the heir?"

"That's what he told me tonight. And he wants to marry me. He can keep me, now, in the style to which I'd like to be accustomed. What do you think of that, Mr. Burke?"

"It sounds like the opportunity of a lifetime. How does Alan know this so soon?"

"Bruce's attorneys arranged to have him released. That alone should be proof. They don't want to lose the account."

From the other end of the table, Larry Puma said, "All right, let's go. We'll do the third act."

Sharon gulped the rest of her coffee as Joe asked her, "And are you going to marry Alan?"

"Not if I get a better offer. And not if it means I'll have to give up my career." She stood up and patted Joe's head. "You wouldn't have a better offer, would you?"

This last question was voiced loudly enough for all to hear. A few heads turned their way, and one of the heads was Norah's. Her face was blank; next to her Leonard Smith was smiling.

Most of them went out to the stage or the auditorium. Joe started to pick up the cups and carry them to the sink. Norah sat at the table, smoking, drinking her coffee, and staring out at nothing.

Joe said, "That Sharon sure uses a lusty perfume."

Nothing from Norah.

Joe started to fill the sink with water. "Alan's the heir, I guess. He asked Sharon to marry him."

"The fool. She'll milk him dry." Norah put out her cigarette and brought her empty cup over to the sink. "I'll wash, if you want."

"No, I don't mind dishwater hands."

He washed; she dried. There was very little dialogue between them. Outside, the dry wind from the east was blowing the litter of the park toward the basketball courts. From the stage, they could hear the voices dimly.

Joe finished the last cup and washed out the sink. Norah hung the towel over the back of a chair and picked up her purse.

"Going?" Joe asked her.

She nodded. "Before I blow up. Or collapse. I've got the blue jitters."

He went over to get his jacket and was going through the pockets for his cigarettes when he heard the door to the patio close.

Norah was walking past the table tennis tables. Joe went over to open the door and call, "You might say good night."

"Good night." She didn't turn.

He closed the door as the door to the prop room slammed from the draft. He watched her through the windows over the counter until she disappeared around the corner of the building.

The wind was howling now, and from somewhere came the clang of an ash-can cover scraping concrete. He poured himself another cup of coffee and sat at the big table.

Women. . . . Interesting and exasperating people, women were, in this man's world. Sharon he could understand; she was a direct girl. She wanted to be a big glamour job in the glamour industry and she meant to get there any way she could make it. Sharon was simple; she thought like a man.

It was actually, Joe reflected, only the nice girls who puzzled him. He probably hadn't known enough of them.

Someone had left a *Theatre Arts* on the table. He leafed through it until he came to a piece by George Jean Nathan. He was deep in the acid of the Nathan prose when he smelled the musky perfume, and looked up.

Sharon was at the counter, getting a cup.

"You must have rubber heels," Joe said. "Where'd you come from?"

"Berkeley. What's *your* home town?"

"A comic, too, eh? How's it going in there?" He went to the stove to lift the heavy pot.

"It's going right along. Don't tell the others, but we're going to be under observation Friday and Saturday nights."

"I don't follow you."

"A man from Paramount on Friday and a scout from Twentieth on Saturday."

"How do you know?"

She smiled at him. "I make it my business to know little things like that. Where's Norah?"

"She went home."

"Oh? Spat?"

"She wasn't feeling well. There is a possibility, then, that an actor might be noticed in one of these productions?"

Sharon sat down and sipped her coffee. "Of course. Why else would I be here? Or Larry Puma, or half a dozen others I could name. The older ones are having fun, but this is just a minor-league showcase for the rest of us." She smiled. "Did you think we were interested in doing something significant and fresh for the 'theeatuh'? Putting on old Broadway stand-bys? We haven't put on an experimental play since this gang started."

"I suppose that's what Alan will do now, start an experimental 'theeatuh'?"

"I suppose. And it'll be the mecca for every fag west of the Rockies. I don't know why those things always wind up as pansy beds, but they do."

"All of them? Even the good ones?"

"All the ones I've ever worked in. And how those swishes loved to cast me as a sexual degenerate."

Joe sniffed and studied a thumbnail.

She laughed. "Don't say it. Bigger men than you have regretted their nasty cracks about little Sharon."

"You know," Joe said, "one thing about you, you're direct. And you don't pretend to be anything you aren't, do you?"

"Only on the stage. Sit down and have another cup of coffee. You're making fascinating conversation."

Joe sat down. "I've had enough coffee. One thing about you I can't completely understand. If it's money you want, why not Alan? Why the career?"

"It—isn't only money. I want to be known. I want to be up there where I can sneer."

There wasn't anything Joe could think of to say to that. The wind screamed, the windows rattled. They sat there quietly.

Leonard Smith came in from the prop room and poured himself a cup of coffee. Sharon looked at him and away; Smith continued to look at her.

Joe felt uncomfortable. He smiled at Smith. "Everything coming along all right?"

"Fine, fine. I have mastered the role of the butler."

Sharon looked up to meet Smith's gaze. "We're bitter tonight, Mr. Smith?"

"Every night," he said. "Older, bitterer. Frustration, you know."

"Frustration? Nice home, single, solvent." Sharon shook her head. "Why should you feel frustrated?"

"I'm not sure you'd understand. But I had hoped to make some small sound before I died."

Joe said, "You're not dead yet, Leonard."

Smith shrugged. "In the way I meant, I'm dead."

Sharon said, "I don't want to make a sound, just a splash."

The windows rattled. A bough from the eucalyptus tree outside rubbed against the roof of the kitchen. All the light in the room seemed to be caught in the red-gold of Sharon's hair.

Smith went over to the sink and rinsed out his cup. "Well, good night, kids. I'm letter perfect, and I'm going home." He went out without looking around.

Sharon lighted another cigarette. "Are you depressed, too?"

"I'm getting that way. I suppose it's a delayed reaction to the murder with all of them. I know looking at corpses used to give me some soul-searching moments. Leonard's past forty, and he hasn't done what he'd hoped—" Joe shook his shoulders. "I don't know. I'm no psychiatrist."

"They all make me laugh," Sharon said. "Slopping through life with no discipline, no goal. And they find themselves forty and empty and go looking for what they missed in a bottle."

"Or a blonde," Joe agreed.

"Or a redhead. Leonard was awful sweet on me for a while."

Joe said nothing. The wind died for a second and they could hear the players on the stage. Sharon rose and went to rinse out her cup.

Her back was to Joe as she said, "Why don't we go some nice place and get drunk?"

Joe wondered if she could hear the pound of his heart. There was a sudden pressure in his loins. He said, "Why not?" and was shamed by the shakiness of his voice.

She turned to look at him speculatively. "You'll be a

gentleman, I hope? I'm not always a lady under alcohol."

He smiled at her. "I'll be as much of a gentleman as I need to be." And he thought, *Stud Burke, at your service, lady. Two times in two nights; that would be a seven-year Burke record.*

It didn't develop along those lines.

They went to the Pico Room of the Shalimar Hotel in Santa Monica and there was dancing. And there were friends of Sharon's, male friends not averse to table-hopping.

They danced with Sharon and he drank. They sat at his table drinking good liquor on his tab and occasionally throwing him a remark as evidence of their good will. Gay, gay, gay: soft lights and sweet music and the finest in bottled bourbon.

Joe got drunk and drunkenly resentful. Around midnight, Sharon rose to dance with a tall and extremely handsome blond young man.

Twenty minutes and five numbers later, they weren't back, and Joe rose to look for them. His legs were unsteady, but he concentrated on keeping his balance and managed to skirt the floor and achieve the French doors that led out to a sheltered patio.

It was too cold for anyone to be out in a patio by this time, but Joe was too drunk to realize that. He went out into the cold, clear night.

They were out there and, to his befuddled vision, they seemed to be standing very close. Perhaps for warmth. Joe called, "What the hell's going on out here?" and saw them turn.

Then it sounded like the man said, "Drop dead," and Joe headed his way.

Sharon said, "Joe, for heaven's sake, don't make a scene here. We were just—"

Joe didn't catch the rest of it. He was close enough now, and he started a right hand from the ground.

It must have been halfway to its intended target when he caught the blond's fist right under the left eye. Joe kept coming in and the next punch the blond threw was the finisher. Joe went back and down and out.

The pounding thunder of a truck seemed to shake the ground and the odor of Sharon's perfume was strong in his nostrils. Filtered sunlight came through the matchstick bamboo drapes that covered the windows running the length of the wall within his view.

He was on a nine-foot davenport in a bright, warm living-room and his head felt like the pit end of a bowling alley. There was a rhythmic pulsation of pain over his eyes and his lower lip was stiff with dried blood. One eye was puffed nearly shut.

Well, he hadn't landed in jail. But he didn't remember coming here. From the fragrance, it must be Sharon's apartment and he remembered somebody telling him that was in the Santa Monica Canyon. The truck that wakened him, then, could have been coming along the Coast Highway.

He rose slowly, painfully and went to look through the bamboo drapes. There was no highway in sight; this place was deeper into the Canyon. On the street below, his car was parked next to the curb.

He tried to remember anything that had happened after the blond's Sunday punch last night. It was a blank. But if this was Sharon's apartment, she had probably driven him here in his car. Though it didn't seem logical that she could handle him alone.

He found the bathroom and examined his face in the mirror. The flesh around the closed eye was puffed and blue. His lip was encrusted with blood but not badly swollen.

"Fool," he said to his image. "Drunken bum." He bathed the lip with warm, soapy water and washed. He rinsed out his mouth and went back to the davenport to lie down again.

The furniture in this room was bright and modern and not cheap. Nor was this a low-rent district. Sharon lived a lot better than her car would indicate. But to her, this was a necessary setting. A car was only transportation, a necessary evil in this town of inadequate public transportation.

Joe rubbed the back of his neck, digging at it, trying to relieve the pain over his eyes.

He heard a sound from the rear of the apartment and then a little later the sound of running water. A few minutes after that, Sharon came into the room.

She was wearing a green flannel robe and mannish slippers. Her lustrous hair was high on her head, and her face looked scrubbed and bright.

"Migawd," Joe said. "You look like you never had a drink in your life."

She stood a few feet from the davenport and gazed down at him gravely.

"You were an awful boor last night."

"I suppose. Who was the blond you were clinching with?"

"We weren't clinching. He's a producer at U-I. He was also a boxer at college, if that's any solace to you."

"It helps. I was drunk. Maybe I'll meet him again."

"I doubt it."

Joe rose slowly to a sitting position. "How did I get here? You certainly didn't carry me."

"I drove the car. You walked to that, with help. And walked from the car to that davenport with my help."

Joe's head was in his hands now, his elbows on his knees. "Who paid the tab?"

"Mr. Crichton, the producer, the one who hit you. Could you drink some coffee, or tomato juice, or something?"

"I can try. I had a look at myself in the bathroom mirror. This Crichton didn't do that with two punches, did he?"

"He must have. Relax. I'll call you when the coffee is ready."

When she called him, there was more than coffee. There were scrambled eggs, light as a cloud, and bacon and spicy tomato cocktail. He discovered he could eat, once the tomato cocktail was down.

By the time he was ready for coffee, he felt almost human again.

He leaned back in his chair and looked at her. "You amaze me. I never figured you for the domestic touch."

"Don't try to figure me, Mr. Policeman. I'm too complex for that. I think I have a chance for a part in a picture at U-I."

"Mmmmm. That's why you were putting the heat to him last night, eh?"

"Maybe. Were you jealous?"

"I was drunk. Although I'd have been just as annoyed if I'd been sober. But I probably wouldn't have started trouble."

"You'd have walked out on me?"

"Probably."

She smiled at him. "Is it too late to apologize?"

He smiled back at her. "No need to. Now that I know it was strictly business. I was thinking just the other day that it's a man's world, and you single girls have a nasty row to hoe."

She looked at him doubtfully. "Was there a crack in there somewhere?"

He shook his head. "Could I have another spot of coffee?"

She poured it and chuckled. "Norah should see us now. What wouldn't she think?"

"She wouldn't think I'd slept in the living-room. By the

way, Norah and I aren't engaged, or anything, you understand."

"I understand, but does she?" Before Joe could answer, Sharon lifted a hand. "You don't know her very well. She can't be casual, not about love. You're the first man in three years that she's shown a definite interest in."

Joe took a breath and said, "She's a great girl."

"Would you like something more to eat?"

"No, thanks. What has Alan told you about his questioning? Does he think the police suspect him more than the others?"

She nodded. "Do you?"

"I don't know. They don't confide in me."

"I didn't mean that. I meant—do *you* suspect him more than the others?"

Joe shook his head. "I don't suspect anyone, yet." He stood up. "Murder isn't my business any more. Well, I'd better get out of here before all your neighbors are up."

"They're all up now," Sharon said. "It's ten o'clock."

The doorbell rang at that moment, and Sharon rose. Joe started to pick up the dishes.

From the other room, he heard Sharon say, "Well, this is a surprise. Come on back and have a cup of coffee."

Joe had turned and was facing the doorway by the time they got there. It was Norah.

Her face was white, and she looked at the dishes still on the table, and then at Joe. He had left his jacket in the living-room; the table was set for two. A girl would need to be very naïve to believe anything good about this tableau.

Norah said quietly, "I saw the car in front, as I was going by. I just wanted to find out for myself."

She turned and went out. The front door slammed.

CHAPTER SIX

Sharon sighed and shook her head. "Now you know. And how innocent it was."

"As it happened," Joe qualified. "Lord, she looked stricken. I can't mean that much to her, not in a few days. She's dramatizing it."

"Maybe. You with your jacket off and I in a robe, breakfast for two—what must the girl think of you?" Sharon paused. "And particularly right after I walked in on the same thing, yesterday. I can understand a tomcat like you, you see. Norah might not."

"I'm not a tomcat, Miss Cassidy. I had some tomcat ideas last night, I'll admit. But generally, I'm a real clean kid. Well, thanks for the breakfast."

"You're welcome." She walked with him into the living-room. "Sorry things worked out as they did."

He chucked her under the chin. "I'll bet you are. See you."

Outside, it was a bright, hot day without wind. He took Channel to the Coast Highway, and the bathers were already parked solidly along here.

At home, he took a hot shower and put on swimming trunks and went out to the patio. There, he connected up the record player and relaxed on a pad in the sun.

The remembrance of Norah's scorn came to him, annoyed him, and disturbed him. Annoyed him, because it implied she had strings on him. And disturbed him because he liked her well enough to value her opinion of him.

She had come into Sharon's place deliberately to spy, which wasn't like her. And Sharon had brought her right back to the kitchen, which *was* like *her*. Joe smiled. That had been a nasty trick of Sharon's, but he couldn't hate the girl like the rest of them did. She was fighting her own battles, without allies. And without whimpering.

His doorbell rang, and he went around to the side of the house to call out, "I'm in the back. Come on back, whoever you are."

It was Alan Dysart. He came along the stepping-stones of the side yard without looking up, watching his footing a little self-consciously, Joe thought.

When he came to the gate, he looked up, and his face was grimly serious.

"Are you alone?"

Joe opened the gate. "All alone. Something **troubling** you, Alan?"

"A number of things."

"Come on in and let down your hair. **Drink?**"

"I don't drink."

Joe indicated a redwood bench and sat down **on the pad.** "You should try it sometime. Great relaxing **influence.** You look all wound up."

"I am. I've been accused of being a murderer and a Communist and practically a queer. And then I drive past Sharon's and see your car there, early this morning, and—" He sat on the redwood bench, leaning forward, his young face taut. "God—"

"Some of the penalties of being artistic," Joe consoled him. "Sharon and I did nothing wrong. Not that I owe you that explanation, but only to keep the record straight. You were kind of pinko in college, weren't you?"

"Who wasn't, in college? I'm a Democrat, now."

"Well, to most of the local papers, that's the same as

being a Commie. Who called you queer?"

"Nobody directly. But the police had me before a psychiatrist and he kept bringing up the woman angle in what he probably thought was subtle interrogation."

"That's standard with artistic people," Joe explained. "It's a compliment, really."

"Not to me. And there's one thing more. How come Larry Puma doesn't get any special attention from the police? He came late; his car was parked on the curve, right next to the slope, there. Larry's *never* late for rehearsal."

"Nobody's being overlooked, Alan. I can guarantee you that. Are you sure you couldn't use a beer? I could."

"Oh, all right—I'm not a teetotaler, exactly. I just don't believe in dulling what intelligence I have."

"One beer won't hurt it much. Drink it from the can?"

Alan nodded, and removed the horn-rimmed glasses. He bent forward over the table, cradling his head in his arms.

When Joe came out with the beer, Alan was sitting erect again, polishing his glasses with a piece of Kleenex. For a non-drinker, he took a healthy first swallow of beer.

Joe sat on the bench on the opposite side of the table. "I understand you're the heir."

"I'm not sure. Who told you? Sharon?"

Joe nodded. "About last night—we went out and had some liquor, and I had too much. Tangled with one of Sharon's friends, and he did this to me." Joe pointed toward his face. "Knocked me cold. I woke up on Sharon's davenport this morning. That's the word on that."

Alan ran a finger along the crimped top of the beer can. "It wasn't any of my business, anyway. I know what she is. It doesn't stop the way I feel about her, but I should know enough not to expect better treatment."

"She's for you, eh?"

The youth nodded. "She is. I fixed up that date with

my uncle for her, too. Sharon *uses* me. She uses everybody."

"But you still love her?"

Alan nodded, and took another sip of beer. "That's not very bright, is it?"

"Brighter men have had softer spots. What have you got against Larry Puma?"

Alan looked up quickly. "Not a damned thing. I wasn't speaking maliciously. The point I was trying to make was that Larry had just as good a chance as I did to kill my uncle. And yet he went out with you and Norah, that night, even before the police had finished investigating."

"It was the mud on your shoes, for one thing," Joe explained. "And you were related and you had to sound off. Nobody likes a loud-mouth."

"No cop, you mean, if you'll pardon the frankness."

"If you'll pardon this frankness—if I were back behind the badge, and you sounded off like you did, I'd have done exactly as Sergeant Krivick did. Who else had a motive?"

"I don't know. My uncle had enemies, plenty of them. He helped to clean out the Reds in two of the Guilds out here. He was an active man and opinionated." Alan took a breath. "And rich."

Joe smiled at him. "Another beer? You killed that one in a hurry."

Alan managed a smile of his own. "Okay. You're not such a bad guy."

"We rich bastards have to stick together," Joe said. "Soon as you get the estate, you'll be voting Republican, too. What country club you going to join?"

"If I'm the heir," Alan said, "I know exactly what I'm going to do with part of the money."

"I'll get the beer," Joe said. "You can tell me about it when I come back."

He came back with the beer and sat down to a one-hour

monologue on the function of truly experimental theater in the current commercial world. Joe understood very little of it, though Alan was plainly trying to phrase it in layman's terms. It still wasn't boring; the intensity of Alan's clear dedication came through better than the words.

When he finally paused for breath, Joe asked, "And you want to establish it out here?"

Alan nodded. "In that house the Players always talk about buying. It would convert beautifully."

"And where will your audience come from? You say only one person in a thousand would appreciate this kind of theater. That gives you an audience of seven people from the Palisades."

Alan took off his glasses as though about to make some important pronouncement. Only his intensity saved the next words from sounding like a pompous absurdity. "If it's as good as I plan it to be, I intend to draw my audience from all of Southern California."

Joe thought of Leonard Smith at that moment, bright, fat little Leonard who wanted to make some small sound before he died. Alan and Leonard, brothers under the skin.

And the rest of them, what motivated them? Working all day, rehearsing all night, receiving not one cent in compensation. Working for a clap of the hand, for a laugh or an appreciative audience murmur? Or something beyond that? Or only infantile exhibitionism?

This wasn't the only area where they struggled or flourished. There wasn't a state in the union that didn't have its quota of amateur theaters. Bright spots in the dark night, interpreting or dulling life, offering barbs or barbiturates, according to the audiences and the aims of each group.

From the bicycle act to the Bard, they were brothers and sisters with one goal—communication with the people at whatever level they could share.

Alan said, "You're mighty quiet. Digesting my polemics?"

Joe stood up. "No. I was thinking of Leonard Smith. He told me he wanted to make some small sound before he died. I was thinking your world is a world of small sounds."

Alan's thin nose twitched and he looked at Joe thoughtfully. "That wasn't bad for a stinking cop. I like that."

"Thanks. How would you go for an omelette? I'm pretty good at making omelettes."

"I'd like one, thank you."

"And one thing more," Joe said. "The way you feel about the theater, that's the way I feel about cops. So kind of lay off the cracks, right?"

Alan was quiet a moment. Then: "Right. I'm sorry, Joe. *Right*."

They were eating when the phone rang. It was Jessup, the cop and part-time realtor. His voice was complaining. "Who's that dame you got climbing in my hair, Joe, this Payne woman?"

"A realtor with a sense of justice," Joe told him. "What's your beef?"

"She threatens to send me up in front of the Board. I don't get it, Joe."

"I could do worse than that," Joe told him. "I could bring you up in front of the Commission. Or come down and kick your fat face in. I hate a crooked cop, Jessup, even after working hours."

"All right. No need to get hot. I'll send you a check. This isn't the first time this has happened out there, Joe."

"It's the first time it's happened to me," Joe said, and hung up.

Back in the kitchen, Alan was smiling. "If you'll pardon the cliché, I couldn't help but overhear. Didn't you call him a 'crooked cop'? Are there such things?" Behind his glasses, his eyes were mocking.

"There are crooked cops," Joe admitted. "And 'crooked lawyers and doctors and actors and priests. Next question?"

"You've answered them all. Well, I've got to run. I enjoyed talking to you, Joe."

"I enjoyed listening. You'll be hanging around the Players, I suppose, as long as Sharon is?"

"I suppose. And you?"

"She's nothing to me," Joe said. "Yet."

"I hope she never is," Alan said earnestly. "For your sake, and mine."

Joe went back out to the patio and the pad. It seemed quieter than it had before Alan came but he couldn't relax. He listened to the record player for a while, and then went in and phoned the Point Realty Company.

Norah was in the office, and he told her, "I wanted to thank you for getting after Jessup. He just phoned."

"You're welcome." Her voice cold.

"It's a nice day," Joe went on. "The beach would be warm."

"I'm sure it would. Was there anything else, Mr. Burke?"

"Yes. *Nothing* happened last night. *Nothing*, except for a fight."

The line went dead.

Women. . . . He picked up a robe and went out to the car. He drove down to the Santa Monica beach, and it was well populated with figures to please any taste. He couldn't shake his mind from thoughts of Norah.

I'm lonely, he told himself, *that's all. No woman could mean this much to me in this short a time if I wasn't lonely. I haven't learned how to loaf.*

He was close to "Muscle Beach" and he could see the over-developed muscular freaks posturing and tumbling, doing handstands and flips or just standing in statuesque poses. Some of them were wrestlers, some beach bums, all of them were ugly with bunched muscle. All of them had a vacuum between the ears.

And yet there were girls watching and applauding, girls as rounded and shapely as the men were bunched and ugly. *Women. . . .*

Woman. Norah, to be explicit. The three-year virgin. The real estate and doughnut seller, painter, amateur actress, set designer. The girl who wouldn't go back to Cedar Rapids.

To hell with Norah.

The girls giggled, the muscle-bound freaks cavorted. The sun burned his back and he turned over, draping a towel over his eyes.

He dozed and dreamed of Sharon alone on a stage, doing a dance that somehow involved a snake. And then the muscle boys were in it, throwing her around like a beach ball. And then, in mid-air, Sharon changed into Norah and he charged in to protest, and one of them threw a handful of sand in his face.

Joe wakened, spitting sand, and saw one of the beach boys bending over to retrieve a ball near by.

Joe sat up and said, "Haven't you freaks got enough beach to play on?"

The man was burned by the sun to a rich brown and his body was muscled right down to his big toes. He held the ball lightly in his finger tips and considered Joe impersonally.

"There are others on the beach, you know," Joe went on. "*Normal* people."

The beach bum smiled easily. "By the looks of your face, you've had enough trouble for one day, major. Simmer down, eh?"

Joe stood up. "I don't think you're man enough to give me any trouble."

For seconds the man considered Joe's two hundred

pounds. Then he said, "You might be right, at that. Sorry, major." He went away.

Next to Joe, a hennaed woman said, "He's just too much of a gentleman to fight with you, sourpuss. You're lucky he is."

Joe looked at the woman and she glared at him.

Joe picked up his towel and slid into his shoes.

The pseudo-redhead said, "Good riddance, sorehead. Don't hurry back."

Joe smiled at her. "You can stop screaming now. The bum can't hear you. And if he could, it probably wouldn't do you any good. I don't think he's got the three dollars."

He left her with her mouth open.

By the time she had regained her voice, he was out of understandable range, though her shrieks were audible. *Women....*

The Chrysler murmured at him, the sun was warm. The sky was blue and clear, the ocean flecked with white. And he was sour. Rich and single and sour; it didn't add.

He went home and dressed and then drove to the playground. Once again he went over the scene from the incinerator to the curved parking area.

He came up to the patio and heard the sound of hammers, and went in through the kitchen to the prop room. Peter Delahunt and Leonard Smith were in there working with saw and hammer.

"Where the hell have you been?" Smith asked him. "We phoned you three times."

"At the beach. Are these the risers?"

"No. Platforms. We have to use our own money. C'mon, you're just the right size to saw some of these two-by-sixes."

They finished a little before six. Pete went home for dinner. Leonard asked Joe, "Any plans for dinner? I'd like a steak."

They washed at the clubhouse and drove over in Joe's

car to Ned's Grille in the Santa Monica Canyon. Ned had steaks for all purses.

Over their pre-dinner drink, Leonard said, "What brought you to the clubhouse? Not that you didn't come at the right time, of course."

"The murder," Joe said. "There's something that bothers me about it, something I should see, but don't."

"You never left the Force, huh?" Leonard said. "Like an old fire horse."

"I suppose. I'm going to work on it. This loafing is something I can't handle right yet. I don't know why it is, but I sure hate an unsolved murder."

"There must be thousands of them." Leonard finished his drink. "Including some that are officially solved."

"Sure. But these tricky ones should be easy. This one looked planned and they're the ones that are usually loaded with leads."

Leonard started to say something and stopped. Joe looked at him curiously.

Leonard smiled. "All right. I'm no informer, but I saw young Dysart rummaging through the incinerator this morning. It probably doesn't mean anything."

"Did he see you?"

"No, I was driving by on Alma. He's the Department's favorite, isn't he?"

"I guess. I'm not sure. He was over to see me this morning. The more I see of him, the less I dislike him. They gave him a bad time, down at the station, I guess. But his uncle's lawyers are working for him now, so they must know he's the heir."

"I thought he might be. A lot of people seem to think that Bruce Dysart hated his nephew as much as his nephew disliked him. That, I happen to know, isn't true. Alan is what Bruce would have been if Bruce hadn't happened to have a great love for the dollar. Alan's *completely* uncompromising. Bruce wasn't."

"Then Alan might guess he was the heir."

Smith frowned. "I wasn't trying to put that construction on my remarks. But I'm sure he knew it."

Joe smiled at Smith. "Okay, Leonard, you've sold me. I'll pick him up in the morning."

"You go to hell," Smith said. "I—kind of like him, too. Though I admit I'm glad the police have somebody besides me they're suspicious of."

There was a rehearsal that night, and Joe went over with Smith. From the clubhouse office, he phoned Krivick at his home.

"I wondered if you'd found the slug," Joe asked him.

"We did. All luck, too. It was in the trunk of that eucalyptus tree on top of the slope."

"Then the shot was fired from below. And at quite an angle. What caliber?"

"Thirty-two. You working on this, Joe?"

"I can't seem to stay out of it. I'd have figured a bigger caliber than that. Ballistics make anything of it?"

"No, it was too battered. You going to be home tonight?"

"No. I'm phoning from the clubhouse. I'll be here. There's a rehearsal tonight."

"Fine. I'll be over. Wait for me there. That Cassidy doll will be there, won't she?"

"Yup."

"Great."

Joe turned from the phone to find Larry Puma standing near one of the desks in the room. Larry said, "Didn't mean to eavesdrop. Had a call to make."

Joe smiled. "You don't need to apologize to me, Larry. I'm not the law."

"You were giving a good imitation of it." Larry went past him and began to dial a number.

In the auditorium, a couple of kids were practicing from the free throw line. Smith and Sharon and Walter

Hamilton were talking in a little group over near the stage.

Outside, that dry, gusty Santa Ana was starting up again. Joe glanced into the kitchen as he went past, but it was dark.

As he joined the group, Sharon made a face at him. "I've been telling them about last night before Norah got a chance to. They don't want to believe we're innocent."

Smith said, "That's what happened to your face. You certainly pack a wallop, Sharon."

Joe could feel himself blushing as they all looked at him. He said, "As long as Norah isn't here, I'll start the coffee." He could hear them laugh as he headed for the kitchen.

He was alone in the kitchen, reading the *Times*, when Krivick came. Joe looked up and gestured toward a chair. "Sit down and have a cup of coffee. You look tired, Sergeant."

"I've been giving this stinking case eighteen hours a day." Krivick slumped into a chair at one end of the table. "That Cassidy girl has *some* history."

Joe was at the stove, pouring the coffee. "I'll bet." He turned to find the sergeant watching him closely.

Then Krivick said, "You know her, don't you? Spent last night with her. Had a fight, too, at the Shalimar, didn't you?"

Joe shook his head. "The other guy had the fight. You've got a man on me, Sergeant?"

Krivick shook his head. "I've been hearing things. Did you know that Cassidy girl was bedded down with Lonnie Goetz for almost two years?"

Joe stared at the sergeant, the cup of coffee motionless in his hand. "Lonnie Goetz? That gun of Brennan's? That—little monster?"

"The same. And there's a rumor that he's been seen around town in the last couple months. Maybe he did a job for her, right?"

Joe set the cup of coffee in front of the sergeant and went to get himself one. "I thought he was dead. I've forgotten the details, but I remember reading some- thing—"

"Look at me, Joe."

Joe turned from the stove to face the sergeant.

Krivick's voice was low. "You wouldn't cover for the broad? She was here, in this room, at the time?"

"I wouldn't cover, Ernie. You know damned well I wouldn't. And neither would the others. None of them like her."

"Okay, then we look for Lonnie. I know what you read, that he'd been killed in an air liner crash. But half the bodies were never identified, and his was one of them." Krivick expelled his breath. "It was a long time ago she was shacked up with him. She was just fifteen when she moved in."

Joe shuddered. "The poor damned kid. Ernie, what did *you* know at fifteen?"

"I knew about violation of the marriage bed. My folks taught me that, and the church."

"But who taught her?"

"I guess nobody, huh? What are you, a bleeder? You sure stopped being a cop awful damned fast." Krivick ran a finger tip around the edge of the coffee cup. "Or maybe you're soft on the doll?"

"Maybe I'm soft on all kids fifteen years old. And you should be, if you're fit to wear the badge."

"You're talking like the *Daily News,* Joe. Save that crap for the women's clubs. A real big man's been murdered."

"Sure, and the *Times* is on your neck."

For seconds there was no dialogue, and then Joe grinned. "I'll apologize if you will."

"All right, you son-of-a-bitch. Watch your tongue, though. Remember when you had to work for a living."

"I'm sorry, Ernie, if I had a brother and he was a murderer, I'd bring him in, even now, off the Force."

"Okay, okay. I watch *Dragnet,* too. But about this plane crash, a few bucks in the right places could change one name on the passenger list, couldn't it? It was just a break, you know. Things were getting hot for Lonnie at the time and he might have wanted to hide in town. The passenger list could have been gimmicked *before* the accident, to make it look like he was simply leaving town. Or it could have been gimmicked *after* the accident, to make it look like he was dead."

Joe frowned. "I'd say it would be damned near impossible *after* the accident. He wouldn't hear about it until long after the papers did, and they'd want the passenger list immediately. How good is this rumor about Lonnie being around town lately?"

"It's a little more than a rumor. A pigeon who's been right more often than wrong."

"Do I know him?"

Krivick shook his head.

"How about flight insurance? Most passengers take that."

"At twenty-five cents for five thousand dollars? Who wouldn't? All but two on this flight did. One of the two was Lonnie."

Joe looked past the sergeant, toward the patio where the kids were playing table tennis. He said, "Sharon ought to be out here any minute."

"I'll wait. How about this young Dysart? Know him well?"

"Not too well. He was over at my house this morning moaning about the way you boys treated him. I like him better than I did at first."

"Pinko, isn't he? One of those intellectual red-hots?"

"I don't know. I guess he was, in college. How can a man tell these days? Young men with any guts are always radical. And suckers for false fronts. The kid claims to be a Democrat now and maybe he is."

"Not my kind of Democrat," Krivick said, "and I've been one all my life."

"And I've voted Republican all my adult life," Joe told him, "and still there are fascists in my party I'd love to read obituaries on. By the American Legion standards, that makes me a Commie, too."

"Not by my standards. Between working for Wallace and fighting fascism, there's a wide stretch of ground, Joe."

Joe shrugged and sipped his coffee. From the stage came the muffled sounds of the players.

Sergeant Krivick was leafing through a notebook. "How about this Norah Payne? She here tonight?"

Joe shook his head.

"Puma?"

Joe nodded.

Krivick held the book open to that page. "I understand that night was the first time he's *ever* been late for rehearsal."

"From Alan Dysart, you understand that. Alan told me that same thing."

"So, you believe him, don't you? You like him more than you used to. He's an honest kid, isn't he?"

"He's no kid and I don't know if he's honest or not. I think he might be too honest for his own good, but I wouldn't bet on it."

"Neither would I. Well, to get back to Puma, do you happen to know where he parked his car that night?"

Joe thought back to the night he and Larry and Norah had left. Larry had taken his car to the Melody Club; where had it been parked? And then he remembered.

He said, "It was parked on the bend, right near the corner of the building. And that seems strange."

"Why?"

"Because that's about the favorite parking spot, and it should have been filled by the time Larry got here."

"Uh-huh. *If* he got here late."

"If he didn't, you'd have learned it by now," Joe thought aloud. "Because the others who came after him would have noticed his car."

"A '46 Ford Tudor? There were three cars here that night close enough to the model to be mistaken for it. Ford didn't change much from '41 to '48, you know. You're sure the car was parked there?"

"I'm sure. I followed him over to Santa Monica."

Krivick asked, "Get the angle I'm working on?"

Joe nodded. "I thought of it myself. Shoot Dysart, dump the gun in the car, and then come in the front door, as though you just arrived."

"Mmmm-hmm. We checked the cars, but we didn't lift the seats, or anything."

"And motive?" Joe asked.

"Oh, yes. Nothing, so far. Two had motive, Alan Dysart and this Cassidy dame. But anybody could have. This could be a political kill, too, you know, Joe. Bruce Dysart was a hard worker against all the Commies in the industry. He had a fine record on that. And he was a powerful man in the business."

"I know. And today Leonard Smith told me something else. He claims Bruce Dysart liked his nephew a lot better than his nephew liked him. Alan could have known that he was the heir."

"I knew that."

Joe asked, "More coffee?"

"I could use some."

At the stove, Joe said, "Are you going to give it to the papers, about Sharon and Lonnie Goetz?"

A few seconds of silence, and then Krivick said, "No."

Joe brought over the cup. "Going soft, Ernie?"

"No. I like kids, too. I'm not like you; I don't make

speeches about it. But I've been active in the Scouts for fourteen years."

Joe coughed. "I—uh—I—"

"You're a professional bleeding heart," Krivick said. "The only thing that keeps me from laughing out loud is your record with the Department."

"You checked that, too, Ernie?"

"Right. When are those uncured hams going to be finished in there?"

"I'll go and find out," Joe said.

But at that moment, Sharon came through the doorway from the prop room.

Joe said, "The sergeant would like to talk to you, Sharon."

She looked from him to the sergeant and back at Joe. "It's not mutual."

Krivick said, "About Lonnie Goetz I'd like to talk, Miss Cassidy. *If* you don't mind."

Again Sharon's glance traveled between them and there was something close to panic in her eyes.

Joe said, "I'll take some coffee out for the others. I'll keep them in the prop room."

"You can stay, if you want," Krivick said.

"I don't want to," Joe told him. "I don't think it's any of my business."

Sharon was still standing stiffly near the doorway, staring at the sergeant when Joe went out with the coffeepot and a carton of paper cups.

He closed the door behind him.

CHAPTER SEVEN

IN THE PROP ROOM, Joe set up some chairs and pushed a couple of make-up tables together. He connected the hot plate and put the huge pot on it and went into the auditorium.

Walter Hamilton and Larry were sitting at a small table in front of the stage, and Joe beckoned to Walter.

When Walter came over, he told him, "Sergeant Krivick is talking to someone in the kitchen. Keep the others out, huh?"

"Sure. Who's the 'someone'? Sharon?"

Joe nodded.

Walter shook his head worriedly. "The police still feel one of us is the—the murderer, then?"

"I don't know, Walter. They can't afford to overlook anything. This case is going to get a lot of Department attention."

"That's to be expected, I suppose. Any ideas on it, Joe?"

"None. I brought the coffee into the prop room."

When he went back to the prop room, he could hear Sharon's voice in the kitchen, and it didn't sound frightened. He heard: "You bastards don't overlook anything, do you? Are you digging back nine years on all the Players?"

Krivick's calm voice: "All the ones with criminal background, Miss Cassidy. When was the last time you saw

Lonnie Goetz?"

A silence, and then: "The last time I talked to him was seven years ago, the day he told me he was getting married."

"And the last time you *saw* him was when?"

"I don't remember. He spent a lot of time in night clubs, and I saw him in places like that, from a distance. But I'm sure I haven't seen him anywhere for five years. He died two years ago, you know."

"I know. Any of his former pals ever look you up?"

"None. That part of my life ended the day Lonnie walked out on me. I thought it was dead and buried. I suppose the papers have this?"

"They won't get it from me, Miss Cassidy. You were seventeen when Lonnie walked out on you?"

"That's correct. You mean, Sergeant, you're *not* giving this to the newspapers? They'd love it, wouldn't they?"

"I don't know, Miss Cassidy. We got the rumor about it, and now you've admitted it. If you hadn't, we'd have no proof you weren't lying. Now that you have admitted it, it would be a crummy trick for me to broadcast it, wouldn't it?"

"I think so. Maybe I got the wrong impression of policemen, living with Lonnie. Sergeant, I apologize for some of the things I called you."

"I'm used to it. Will you tell that Mr. Puma to come in next?"

"With pleasure."

Joe was bending over the coffeepot like a non-eavesdropper when Sharon opened the door.

"I'll take some of that," she said, and leaned against a battered davenport. "Who else was listening?"

"Nobody. Nobody else and nobody. Though I'll bet it would make interesting hearing." He poured her a cup of coffee and brought it to her.

She took it and nodded her thanks. She sat down on

the davenport. "That sergeant in there isn't typical, is he? He seemed nice."

"He's typical. He's very active in the Boy Scouts. A good man, in my professional opinion."

Sharon frowned. "Oh, he wanted me to tell Larry Puma to come in now. Would you do that for me? I don't want Larry to think— Well, would you?"

Joe was already on the way to the auditorium.

When he came back, and Larry had gone into the kitchen, Sharon asked, "Did the sergeant tell you about Lonnie, too?"

"Lonnie who? I didn't even know we had a Lonnie in the Players."

Sharon's smile was scornful. "Stick with the coffee, Joe. You're no actor. So he did tell you?"

"Cream?" Joe asked. "Sugar?"

"Neither, thanks. I was fifteen when I met Lonnie. I was seventeen when I left him. Or he left me, rather. You'd be surprised at the people Lonnie knew, Joe. And what he knew about them."

She learned about life from Lonnie, Joe thought. *Just like in the soap operas.* He said nothing.

Sharon's voice was low. "He knew producers and oil men and some of the best people in town."

"Some of the worst people from the best families, you mean," Joe corrected her. "I was a cop a long time, Sharon. I'm not real bright, but I know the kind of people you mean. Some of our *biggest* movie stars, but none of our best. Some of the our richest citizens, but none of our sound ones. And all the degenerate misfits from the otherwise fine families. You left Lonnie, but you never left his viewpoint."

"Yes, grandpa. The world is bright and clean and nothing pays off like virtue and thrift."

Joe said nothing, burning slightly.

Sharon said, "You'd have wound up with big feet and

a small pension if your aunt hadn't died. Don't drown me in your platitudes, Dick Tracy."

"Okay. Get off my back. Who can tell *you* anything?" Joe heard the feet of the players coming down the steps and he started to pour the coffee.

Gabble, gabble, gabble and the smoke of half a dozen cigarettes. Friendly people and fairly bright chatter, but no warmth for Joe. Because Norah wasn't there? Or because Sharon had been so cynical?

Sharon said little. More than once Joe looked over to find her eyes on him. Once she made a face at him.

Then the door from the kitchen opened, and Larry Puma came through it. He said, "Leonard next."

Leonard looked surprised for a second, and then he gulped the rest of his coffee and went through the door. He closed it behind him, and there was a moment's silence in the prop room.

Larry went over to the coffeepot and poured a cup for himself. He came over to sit next to Joe. "What's this business about the parking? What does it mean?"

"I don't know. Where did you park?"

"The night of the murder? On the bend in front. Somebody was pulling away as I came in and there was a hole, so I grabbed it."

"You wouldn't remember who was pulling away?"

"I don't even remember what kind of car it was. That sergeant is sure making a production out of it, though." Larry rubbed the back of his neck. "Hell, I never even knew the man. Smith and Sharon are the only ones in the gang who knew him."

"And Alan," Joe added. "I wonder if he'll turn out to be the heir."

"Naturally. That's his kind of luck." Larry finished his coffee and rose. "All right. Everyone who's in the second act, let's go."

About half of them went up the steps to the stage. Then

Leonard Smith came out from the kitchen and asked, "Is Norah here?"

Joe shook his head.

"Alan Dysart?"

"I haven't seen him."

"Well, I guess he wants you then, Joe. Put in a word for us." Leonard smiled and went up the steps.

In the kitchen, Krivick was writing something in a notebook. He looked up and asked, "Any more of that coffee around?"

"I'll bring you a cup."

When Joe brought the coffee, Krivick was standing near the windows, looking out at the now dark patio. When Joe closed the door, Krivick turned and came over to the table. He pulled a cigarette package from his jacket pocket and saw that it was empty. He crumpled it.

Joe slid his pack along the table. "Well, Ernie?"

"Nothing. Not a stinking, logical lead. This thing could be political, Joe. Dysart got a lot of poison pen letters when he helped to clean up the Screen Writers' Guild."

Krivick lighted one of Joe's cigarettes and inhaled deeply. He leaned back in his chair and rolled his head, loosening the neck muscles. In the bright kitchen light he looked gray and old.

Joe said, "Nobody loves a rich man. It could be anybody."

Krivick said nothing, staring moodily out toward the dark patio.

"Something will break," Joe consoled him. "There are probably two or three people who know something they haven't told you. It will fester in them, and things will begin to add up."

"Maybe. In a month, a year. The Department wants action on this one. I even looked into the possibility of that Dial Forest, that writer, having something to do with it."

"You mean the one Bruce was trying to beat down, the man who wrote *Week End Widow?*"

"That's the man. He couldn't have had a better alibi. He was in the Beverly Hills clink on a drunken driving charge at the time."

"You've still got Lonnie Goetz."

"I've got the Lonnie Goetz rumor. Well, I'll work on that tomorrow. I've got to get *some* sleep." He pushed his chair back and stood up. "Keep me informed, Joe, if you latch on to anything."

"Of course. And don't brood, kid. Easier cases have gone unsolved."

"I know. But I was up for promotion. Be seeing you." He went out through the door that led to the auditorium.

Eight hours a day was all the Department required, but Krivick was putting in a lot of his own time. One of those soft political jobs indignant taxpayers were always screaming about. And he'd wind up, as Sharon had phrased it, with big feet and a small pension.

And the memory of an adult lifetime spent looking at the ugliest side of man.

The door from the patio opened and Alan Dysart came in. He said, "I saw the flatfoot, so I waited until he left. I still can't get to like the odor of cop."

"Shut up," Joe said.

Alan stared at him. "I—"

"Just keep your goddamned mouth shut. You're a real bright kid, but you've got a lot of things to learn."

"I apologize. Is there any coffee?"

"In the prop room."

Alan went through the doorway, his thin face taut, his tall body stiffly resentful. In a moment, Joe heard him talking to someone and from the stage he heard Sharon's warm voice.

Then Alan came back in, a cup of coffee in his hand,

a tentative smile on his face. "I remember you warned me. My apology was sincere."

"And accepted. You so-called 'liberals' give me a pain in the ass, at times. You bleed for the common man—until you meet one. And then you loathe him. Krivick's bringing up three daughters on his crummy pay. Working overtime without getting paid for it and putting in any other conscious moments working for the Boy Scouts. He takes your adolescent scorn and still remains a registered Democrat. I'd call that *balance,* and it's maybe something you could start learning."

"I'm sorry, Joe. What else do you want me to say? You don't have to make like McCarthy."

"It's lippy pseudo-liberals like you who make otherwise decent people support McCarthy."

"That I won't accept. And you don't believe it, either. It's fear and sick minds that make monsters like him possible."

"And what makes monsters like Stalin possible?"

"The secret *police.* It's a *police* state. Now tell me to shut my goddamned mouth again. That 'word' is out."

Joe started to say something and stopped. Then he said, "I apologize for the nasty things I said, but not the gist of it." He reached over for his package of cigarettes, still on the table where Krivick had left it. Casually he asked, "Why were you rooting through the incinerator this morning?"

Alan smiled. "I was playing detective. It would be a logical place to get rid of a gun, wouldn't it?"

"No. Any theories on the kill?"

"None I'd care to voice. It's a rather far-fetched theory, and too silly to mention, probably. Have you any, Mr. Burke?"

Joe shook his head, and stood up. "I've had enough for one day. I'll be seeing you."

"Good night, Joe."

Joe went out through the auditorium and stopped for a moment to watch Sharon deliver a few lines. The opening was for Thursday night and they'd be ready. The play was flowing, making communication now. There were four players on the stage, but the eye was attracted to Sharon, no matter who was talking. The male eye, at any rate.

Outside, Joe paused a moment in front of the wide door, looking out at the lights on the hills and the few lights still visible in the quiet town. Behind him he could hear the voices of the players through the closed door.

Small sounds in the dark night. Small sounds on a bright stage while the citizens slept, storing strength for their dull tomorrows. In the desert of darkness an oasis of the dedicated preparing a week-end illusion for the nominal price of seventy-five cents. Magic, at six-bits a head.

Shoe clerks and housewives, embryonic artists and defeated vaudeville troupers, hams and hacks and the hopeless, working together toward a salable illusion. And out here, in the Celluloid center, the chance that it might not be in vain. Scouts did come to these performances; professionals from the studios did work in them. On a clear day, you can see MGM.

The Chrysler's hundred and eighty horses came to life and Joe steered the big car past the dark houses along the dimly lighted streets. He felt slightly ashamed of his outburst against Alan Dysart. The kid was in rebellion against the established order, a standard enough attitude for the young and intelligent and sensitive. Dysart would settle down. He might not ever be able to compromise but he'd learn to adjust to the inevitable.

It had been a bad day. It hadn't been too bad a day until Norah had walked into Sharon's kitchen this morning and found him there. Well, nothing had happened. If Norah wanted to believe something had happened, that was her privilege. Nothing had.

A small voice at the back of his mind said, *Not because you didn't want it to, sexy.*

"Nothing happened," Joe said aloud. "A fact's a fact."

The small voice said nothing.

"I'm a single man," Joe continued. "Single, single, single. I'm not even engaged. Nobody's got any strings on me, understand?"

The small voice chuckled.

"To hell with all women," Joe told it. "Trouble, that's all they are. Except Aunt Selena, and she's dead."

And I'm rich, he thought, *and why shouldn't I be happy? What the hell am I growling about?*

He put the car in the garage, went into his dark house, and turned the TV to the eleven o'clock news.

There was little news that day and the commentator's labored effort to make something out of nothing was irksome. The only other program of even passing interest was a movie of comparatively recent vintage, starring Milton Sills. He snapped the set off and went out into the kitchen, to rummage the refrigerator.

It contained two dried-out radishes and half a quart of milk. He made cocoa and found some bread to toast and there was an unopened jar of peanut butter.

Outside, the mellow tones of a hot-rod's double tail pipes went by on Via. Inside, the refrigerator hummed and the furnace fan squeaked lazily and the leaky faucet went *drip, drip, drip* in the kitchen sink.

He thought of Norah and Sharon, Alan, Larry, Leonard, Walter, Pete Delahunt, and Lonnie Goetz. He thought of Dick Metzger, which brought him back to Norah. There wasn't any reason she should attend the rehearsal tonight, but he wondered if she'd stayed away because of this morning's discovery.

He thought of phoning her, but she might be asleep now, and tomorrow would do as well.

Lonnie Goetz. . . . There was a name that made sense in the murder. There was a man trained to kill without motive beyond the pay. Joe wondered who'd given Krivick the word on Lonnie Goetz.

Joe had a few pigeons of his own, one of whom traveled in the circles formerly traveled by Lonnie. He glanced at the clock over the sink; it was 11:20. Maybe?

He found the number in his old notebook and called it. A woman answered.

"Vera?" Joe asked.

"Speaking."

"This is Joe Burke. Your boy around?"

"He's due any minute, Joe. What's this I hear about you?"

"You tell me."

"I hear you hit the jackpot and retired. You're loaded, I heard."

"That's about it. How's your boy treating you?"

"All right. Why? Are you making conversation, Joe, or are you really interested? Because I'm always open to an offer. Arty doesn't ring the bells in me he used to."

"I'm kind of tied up, right now," Joe told her. "But I'll remember you're available. Where is Arty?"

"Business, he said, but that could mean anything with him. I got a feeling I don't make music in him any more, either. You're not married, Joe?"

"No. Was it marriage you had in mind, Vera?"

"If you're really loaded. Oh, here's the big man now."

Some low dialogue between them and then Arty's voice: "Making time with my girl, Joe?"

·   "Not enough. Arty, I heard a rumor."

"So?"

"That Lonnie Goetz was alive and in town."

"I didn't hear it. You're not with the Department any more, are you, Joe? You set up as a shamus?"

"No, this is just personal, Arty. It would be worth a

hundred for me to know for sure, though."

A silence, and then: "I think I could find out. I'm kind of chummy with some of his old buddies. I'll phone you, Joe. Same number?"

"No." Joe gave him the new one. And asked, "Still making book?"

"Here and there. Don't tell me *you're* playing the ponies?"

"I will be. Very boring life, being a rich man. Phone me when you get the word."

Joe went back to the kitchen and washed the knife and spoon and cup and the cocoa pan. He wasn't sleepy; he went into the study and picked up one of the books on little theater he'd brought from the library.

But he continued to think of Lonnie. If he was alive and implicated in the murder, that would implicate Sharon. Sharon had the motive, Lonnie the gun. He put the book down and went into the bathroom to run some hot water into the tub.

He soaked in the water until it started to cool and then went to bed. And to sleep.

The climate had changed by morning, back to the gray chill that was expected that time of the year. He drove to the center and ate his breakfast at the drugstore.

Smith came in while he was waiting for his eggs and took the stool next to Joe. "I see our good weather has gone."

Joe nodded.

Smith sat down and unfolded a copy of the *Times*. "That Sergeant Krivick isn't getting anywhere with this case, is he?" He indicated the first-page story under a subhead. "Even the paper hasn't any new rumors this morning."

"A case can crack any time," Joe told him. His eggs arrived and he started to eat.

"You're not very friendly this morning," Smith said.

"Is it because I'm one of the suspects?"

"No, Leonard. I've been gloomy since yesterday. That murder has me down, I guess. There's a hole in this thing as big as my head and I can't find it."

"How do you know there's a hole in it, then?"

"Hunch. I don't know. Something bothers me about it."

Smith yawned and turned a page of the paper. "Well, you're not being paid to work on it, are you?"

"No. But I'm not doing anything else of importance."

"We're building a set this afternoon. You can help with that if you're so ambitious."

"Maybe I will," Joe told him. "There are some people I have to see first, though. I might not be through in time."

The first person he had to see was Norah, but she wasn't at the office. She was taking a few days' vacation and the girl in the office didn't know where she was spending them.

He went from there to Hollywood, to a dim and dusty tobacco store on Ivar. It was less dim and not nearly as dusty now; it had gone through a change of management. The new owner actually sold tobacco.

Joe drove from there to Beverly Hills, to one of the showplaces off Sunset Boulevard. He was stretching a thin friendship to its cracking point coming here with questions, but it was his best hope.

He'd known the occupant of the house before he'd gone respectable; Joe had saved his daughter from marrying a man even less admirable than her father. The old man had expressed his appreciation for that. But the old man might resent acting as a pigeon.

To the butler at the door, Joe said, "I'd like to see Mr. Brennan. You can tell him it's Joe Burke calling."

The butler was back in less than a minute. "This way, sir."

Joe followed him through the entrance hall to another

hall which ran through the center of the house. Through a closed door at the end of this hall, Joe heard the *spat* of a small-caliber weapon.

The butler opened the door. "Mr. Brennan will see you here, sir."

Joe went in and the door closed behind him. It was a narrow room. At the far end there were a number of targets such as are used in small-caliber shooting galleries. At this end of the room, Ray Brennan was standing, sighting a .22-caliber target pistol.

There was another *spat* and one of the smaller ducks at the far end flipped over. Brennan continued to load and shoot, working the entire row of ducks.

He must have been over sixty but his white hair was full and lustrous and his tanned face unlined. And there wasn't any doubt as to the steadiness of his hands. This was a *rifle* range; Brennan was using a *pistol*.

He turned finally, and smiled at Joe. "Pardon the theatrics. I was rude, I know, but I wanted to impress you."

"You did," Joe admitted. "That's sweet shooting, Mr. Brennan."

"Thank you." Brennan was running a swab through the barrel now. "I see by the papers you've retired, Joe."

"You must read carefully; it didn't get much ink."

"I read them carefully. And watch television faithfully and practice here every morning. I'm retired, too, Joe."

"I know."

Brennan put the gun on a small table near by and picked up another. "Social call, Joe?"

"No. Just checking a rumor."

Brennan looked up, waiting.

"About Lonnie Goetz," Joe went on. "I heard he was alive and in town."

Nothing showed on Brennan's face. "Checking for whom, Joe?"

"For me, so far. For the law eventually."

"And why come to me?"

"Because you'd know. He was working for you, wasn't he, about the time he was supposed to have died?"

"Maybe. There aren't any feathers on me, Joe."

"I know that. It's one of the reasons I hesitated about coming here. Do you remember a girl named Sharon Cassidy, Lonnie's girl?"

Brennan shook his head. "Where did you hear this about Lonnie being alive?"

"From the police, who probably got it from somebody with feathers." Joe smiled. "Sorry to have bothered you, Mr. Brennan." He turned toward the door.

"Just a moment," Brennan said quietly, and Joe turned back.

"Lonnie's dead," Brennan said flatly. "I know it. I watched him get on the plane."

"Thanks. I appreciate it."

Brennan nodded. His smile was thin. "Drop in any time, Joe. But *never* with questions again. Fair enough?"

"Fair enough, and thanks again."

Brennan nodded. He was sighting the new gun now. Joe heard the *spat* as he closed the door. In the entrance hall, the butler was waiting to open the front door for him.

So quiet, so dignified, so upper class. And all built on the narcotics trade. But then, there were bigger houses in the town built on the patent medicine trade, which was considered legitimate.

At the super-market in the Palisades, Joe stocked up on meat and frozen vegetables, eggs, fruit juice, breakfast food, and canned soup.

It was nearly two now and he broiled one of the steaks he'd bought and made a sandwich of it. That, with a glass of milk, was his lunch.

Then he phoned the station but Krivick wasn't there,

nor was he at home. Joe put on some working clothes and went down to the clubhouse.

Hamilton and Leonard Smith were there, pulling some flats out of the small shed that opened off the prop room. The flats they were choosing were a hideous shade of green.

"Damn it," Smith said. "I wish Norah were here. These should be painted today, if we get them up."

"I can paint," Joe volunteered.

"We can all paint," Smith said, "but who can mix the colors we want? I've seen some of your sport shirts, so that eliminates you. Norah's the girl with color sense."

"Couldn't you get her at the office?" Walter asked.

Smith shook his head. "She's taking a few days' vacation." He looked steadily at Joe. "I don't know why. Do you, Joe?"

"Shut up and let's get to work," Joe said.

Walter, oblivious to it all, said, "She's certainly the number-one worker around here. I shudder to think of how little we'd accomplish without her."

"Exactly," Smith said. "I'd rather have *anybody* in the organization quit before she did."

Joe was bending over, trying to extricate a flat. He stood erect now and looked at Smith. "Nothing personal in that, Leonard?"

Smith didn't answer.

Walter paused to look at them. "What the hell goes on here?"

Smith smiled. "I'm sorry. I was needling Joe and I now realize it wasn't all in fun on my part. I apologize, Joe."

Joe grinned at him and winked.

Hamilton said, "If I'm not too young to know, what has Norah's absence got to do with Joe?"

"Nothing," Joe said. "Leonard was guessing and guessing wrong."

Smith shook his head. "I've watched her and admired

her for a long time. I'm not likely to be wrong about Norah."

"Let's drop the subject," Joe suggested, "and get to the work at hand."

"I'll second that," Smith said.

They went to work, and while they worked they talked. Joe learned about ground rows and sill irons, about lash cleats and brace cleats, corner blocks and lash lines. He learned the difference between scenery linen, enameling duck, and muslin, between gauze and scrim, between a drop and a border.

At five-thirty his stomach was growling at him, but they still had a full hour's work ahead of them. Neither of the other two made any comments about being hungry; Joe worked uncomplainingly on.

A little after six-thirty Walter said, "Well, that should just about do it. I'll admit none of us is a Bel Geddes, but I think we've shown a certain esthetic flair."

"Would you translate that for me?" Joe asked.

"He means he's seen worse," Leonard said. "I'm trying to remember if I have."

The big door at the far end of the auditorium opened then, and they all looked that way.

It was Norah.

"Greetings," Hamilton called. "I thought you were out of town."

"I was, but I remembered about the set and what a horrible sense of color Leonard had."

"Thank you," Leonard said. "Hope we didn't interrupt anything? Like a rendezvous in some glamorous desert watering place?"

Joe said, "I think I left a hammer back of that fireplace. I'd better get it before we forget it."

There wasn't any reasonable reason why his heart should pound, or his knees suddenly turn to butter. He was hungry, of course, but he'd been hungry before.

He went around the edge of a wing and squirmed his way through the narrow passage between the wing and the side of the stage.

He heard Leonard call, "Watch it, Joe—" and then he felt the pain right above his ear. He was conscious of the ripping sound of the scenery linen just before the lights went out. . . .

CHAPTER EIGHT

No VISIONS IN THE BLACKNESS, but the smell of Norah's perfume and then a drop of moisture on his cheek and he opened his eyes.

Norah's face was above him; his head was in her lap. She was sitting on the stage and she was crying; it was her tear on his cheek.

"Hello," he said. "Stop crying."

She sniffed and rubbed both her eyes with the back of one hand. "You stupid, vulgar Irishman."

He smiled. "Want a cigarette?"

Over Norah's shoulder, Hamilton was looking down anxiously. "Are you all right, Joe? Leonard's gone for the first-aid kit. Can you get up all right?"

Joe grinned at him. "Why should I? Would you?"

"You're bleeding," Norah said. "It's quite a gash, Joe."

He sat up quickly. "On your skirt? I'll ruin it, honey."

Smith was back now with the kit. "God, I'm sorry, Joe. I just remembered, when you started back, that I'd left a hammer up on that wing. The claw must have—" Leonard stopped, looking sick.

Norah said, "I'll handle it, Leonard. You'd better get some air. Let's go into the kitchen where we can wash this, first. And I'll want scissors, Walter. We'll have to cut away some of the hair."

Walter, too, was looking pale. "I know where there's a pair." He went away.

Smith still stood there, looking bleakly at both of them.
Norah asked, "Shall I help you up, Joe?"

He shook his head and got slowly to his feet. There was
very little pain, but perhaps that would come later. Smith
looked at him a second before turning and going down
the steps to the auditorium.

Norah said quietly, "Leonard is acting strangely, isn't
he?"

"He's goofy for you," Joe said. "I guess I am, too, honey."
Joe looked at her skirt, spotted with blood, and up to meet
her gaze. "I love you, Norah."

A faint color in her cheeks. "Let's not be too gallant,
just because I've— Let's get into the kitchen." She jostled
his arm. "Come on."

Walter was in the kitchen when they got there and he
had blended the water in the swing faucet to the proper
temperature.

Norah worked quickly and gently and finished by putting a pad of gauze over the cut. She said, "I think you
should see a doctor, Joe. It might need a few stitches. I
think we can get Doctor Gendron at home."

"I want to eat first. I'm dying of hunger. Are we friends
again?"

She nodded.

He lifted her chin. "No more than that?"

Her gaze met his and dropped. "I don't know. I want
to be *sure,* Joe. Some things in you— You're— Oh, I don't
want to talk about it now."

"I'm dumb, huh? And vulgar."

"I don't believe you're either. Please—" She took a
breath. "I don't want to sound like Elsie Dinsmore. Let's
drop it for now, Joe?"

"All right. Have you eaten?"

She nodded. "I could use a cup of coffee, though." She
put a hand on Joe's arm. "Ask Leonard to come along.
We can go to Ned's Grille; you two won't need to change

for that."

"All right. You like him, don't you?"

She nodded, and flicked Joe's nose with a forefinger. "I like him."

He found Leonard out on the patio, smoking a cigarette. He asked, "How about going to Ned's, Leonard? I'm starving."

"Fair enough. Are we going to paint the set after that? We should."

"I'm willing. We'll talk it over with Norah."

Leonard dropped his cigarette and stepped on it. He didn't look at Joe as he said, "It's been a bad afternoon. That hammer business didn't make it any happier. Joe, I'm sorry. I'm rather—pathological about Norah. But I know you'll treat her right."

"Don't be playing cupid, Leonard. Let's get cleaned up."

Hamilton was going home for dinner; he agreed to come back for the painting.

It was a quiet meal. Joe's head was beginning to throb a little and Norah and Smith couldn't seem to find any conversational topics worth expanding.

Norah had phoned Doctor Gendron from Ned's; Joe drove to the doctor's home after dropping Norah and Smith at the clubhouse.

The cut required seven stitches, and the doctor told Joe, "You're not the first casualty the Players have sent over. You people certainly earn the money you don't get."

Joe kept a straight face as he said, "There's no sacrifice I wouldn't make for my art."

Doctor Gendron finished without further dialogue.

At the clubhouse, Norah donned a paint-spattered smock and was mixing a yellowish chartreuse in a huge bucket. Hamilton was painting a cabinet a chocolate brown.

Joe stayed with it as long as he could. But the smell of

paint increased the throbbing ache of his bruised head and he had to quit before they were finished.

He sat at the rear of the auditorium and watched the flats become a room. When they were almost finished, Joe went to the kitchen. He found a quarter pound of coffee and put one of the big pots on to heat.

The coffee was ready by the time they'd cleaned the brushes and the buckets and themselves. Norah came into the kitchen and sniffed. "That's a finer aroma than we've had the last few hours. How's the head?"

"It aches steadily, but it doesn't seem to be getting worse. When do we set up the furniture?"

"Tomorrow, I suppose. We open Thursday. There's nothing new on the murder? At least there isn't in the papers."

"Nothing new that I know of," Joe told her.

Then Hamilton and Smith came in and Joe poured the coffee.

Walter said, "The advance ticket sale is the best we've ever had. And the play isn't very well known. Amateur Hawkshaws, I suppose."

"As long as they pay," Norah said, "who cares *why* they're here?"

Walter sipped his coffee. "I do. We can't arrange for a murder every month. Sharon's right about this play, you know. It's very weak. Larry's saved it with his directing, but I'm sorry we ever chose it."

"Larry wanted it," Smith pointed out. "All these amateur directors favor something they've handled before. I think, from now on, we should choose the play and *then* look for a man to direct it."

Hamilton smiled. "And look and look and look. You know how arbitrary they can be, Leonard."

"Because we baby them."

"Probably. Because we need a good man who'll work for nothing. And if we don't give him what he wants, there are a dozen other amateur groups within shouting distance who will." Hamilton sighed. "Considering all the limitations we have, I think we're lucky to have lasted as long as we have."

"I can give you one reason for that," Smith said. "Or two, rather. You and Norah are willing to do all the dirty work so some of these young snips can show off for their relatives. In any amateur group, it's the people like you and Norah who keep it going."

Norah bowed. "Thank you, kind sir. And add the name of a man called Leonard Smith." She inclined her head toward Joe. "Not to mention our apprentice on the sucker list, Hole-in-the-Head Burke."

Joe raised his cup high. "To all of us."

They drank solemnly.

Norah said, "All those years on the Force, and Joe hasn't a scar. A few days after he meets us, he's knocked out by a producer and then has his scalp laid open with a hammer."

They laughed.

Joe asked, "Who told you the man was a producer? Have you and Sharon been talking?"

Norah smiled coolly. "No, dear. I inquired around a bit."

Smith rose and said, "Good night, people. I've had a full day."

"And I," Walter said. He, too, rose. "Joe, when you decide to invest that money of yours, remember Walter Hamilton and Associates."

They went out, and Joe looked at Norah. "Still gloomy?"

"Some. It wasn't just that Sharon business. It was Dysart's death, too. Do you ever think of death, Joe, of *your* death?"

"Once in a while. And then I tell myself it isn't that important, I'm not that important. Everybody dies. Think of all those who've gone ahead of us, Norah."

"I think of them. I think of my father. But Joe, they died *believing*."

"Oh. And you don't?"

"No. Do you?"

"I don't know. Have a cigarette."

She took one and he held a light for her. She said, "I used to get by with that Stevenson bromide, that 'Glad did I live and gladly die, And I laid me down with a will.' But not any more. And if there's no tomorrow, what am *I* leaving behind?"

Joe thought of Smith's "some small sound." He said, "You could leave some kids. I'd be glad to help you with that."

She studied him. "Were you trying to be funny?"

"No. What am I leaving behind? What am I contributing, for that matter, while I'm here? And there are millions like us, Norah, leaving nothing but their kids as contributions. We should get married."

She shook her head. "That isn't a good enough reason. I still feel that I have *some* talent I should develop. I feel so wasted."

"You can still develop it, married to me. I can afford a talented wife."

She smiled. "You must like me. We'd better go. I imagine the place will be locked up soon."

"Why don't we go to my house?" Joe suggested. "I've some records I don't appreciate. You can explain them to me."

She smiled wryly. "What, no etchings?"

"Now who's vulgar? It wasn't what I had in mind, honestly."

"It must have been in my mind, then. All right, here we go."

The night was cold and gusty, but the stars were clear and the moon bright. Joe followed Norah's car over to the parking lot behind the Point Realty Company, where she left it.

She climbed into the Chrysler all huddled up. "Cold, cold, cold. Isn't there a heater in this monster?"

"I don't know if the water's warm enough yet. We'll be warm in a few minutes. I've some Old Forester in the cupboard."

"Don't flaunt your wealth. Joe, if there was something about the murder you knew, would you keep it from me?"

"Sure. I'd keep it from everybody but the Department. It's my training."

"But you do know something, don't you? About Sharon."

"Maybe. Do you?"

"A few things. Joe, that's why you went with her the other night, isn't it? It was sort of an—investigation?"

He hesitated for seconds before he said, "No."

"You don't have to be so honest. You could leave a girl a few illusions."

"What are the 'few things' you know about her?"

"Nothing I mean to tell you, policeman."

His garage door was open, and he pulled right in. They went through the breezeway from there to the kitchen, and Joe snapped on the light.

"You turn up the thermostat," Norah said. "I'll mix the drinks."

Joe set up the thermostat and then went into the den to put records on the player. He put on the Philadelphia's recording of the *Mathis der Maler Symphony* and waited for the instrument to warm up.

Norah came in with the drinks, just as the first record dropped. She stood there a few seconds and then said, "Not Hindemith. Joe, you can't go from Berlin to Hindemith and if you do, I can't show you the way. Haven't you anything a little closer to my level?"

"Chopin," he said, "but even I enjoy that. I figured it must be low-brow."

She shook her head. "He was the greatest in his field, but it was a limited field. How about something we both enjoy?"

He frowned. *"Porgy and Bess?"*

She looked doubtful.

He grinned. "Well, I've got Goodman's 1938 concert at Carnegie Hall."

"Put it on," she said. "Don't waste any time. I haven't heard it for a week, and then on my little scratch box."

They had it with their first drinks. Outside, the wind had grown stronger. In the den, it was warm and the great ones from the stage of Carnegie Hall were pouring out their uninhibited challenges.

And after that, for a change of mood, some of George Shearing's light and sophisticated touch.

Norah said, "Either this is strong whisky or I'm particularly susceptible tonight."

"I'll drive you to your car if you're tired."

"Well—" she said, and looked at him, her head to one side.

He kept his face blank. "And there's food. I stocked up today. Are you hungry?"

She continued to study him. "You knew this would happen, didn't you? Alcohol did it last time, and you knew if— You are a dog, Joe Burke."

"Here we go again," he said. "You're talking yourself into a state of mind. I haven't laid a finger on you."

"So," she said, "who's stopping you?"

In the morning, he wakened first this time and he stood for a moment next to the bed, looking down at her. She looked peaceful and beautiful and young in repose. She was on her back and her long, slim body made a narrow ridge under the covers. She would be all he'd want for the rest of his life.

He went into the kitchen to put water on for coffee.

Through the window over the sink he could see it was another of those out-of-season, sunny, dry days. This should be a new winter record.

He was in the bathroom, shaving, when she went down the hall to the other bathroom. He had the orange juice poured and the bacon draining on toweling paper when she came out to the kitchen.

She stood behind him and put her arms around him. "I'm a tramp. But I feel wonderful."

"You are wonderful."

"I'm a beast. I never even thought of your poor, cut head."

"Neither did I. When are we going to get married?"

"You want to buy milk when you own a cow?"

He turned around. "Don't talk like that. It's not like you."

"It's like you, though, isn't it? I want to be like you."

"I don't. I want you to be like you. It's *you* I love. How do you want your eggs?"

She smiled, and tweaked his nose. "In bed. Don't be stuffy, Joe. It's such a beautiful day and it was such a beautiful night. I'll fix the eggs. We'll pretend we're married."

"We're not married. I'll handle the eggs."

"Yes, master." She went over to the nook and sat down. She sipped her orange juice and opened the *Times*. "I like my eggs scrambled."

He was beating them when she said, "Nothing about the murder on the front page. I suppose there's nothing new."

"I suppose." He added a little cream and finished beating the eggs. "You can put some bread in the toaster." He put the eggs on the griddle. "Where'd you go yesterday?"

Silence. He turned to look at her and found her staring at him. She said, "You sounded exactly like a policeman when you asked that."

"I didn't mean to. I meant to sound like a lover, or husband."

"Well, then, I started for La Quinta, but changed my mind. And what did *you* do, yesterday?"

"Looked up some of my criminal friends. Learned something, too." He brought over her eggs and a few strips of bacon.

"Thank you, sir. Learned something. About Sharon?"

"Maybe. What made you guess that?"

"Who else among the Players ever had any criminal friends?"

"I don't know. You tell me." He brought over his own eggs and sat across from her.

"I knew a few," she said. "You can't gad about Hollywood for very long without getting to know a few." She paused. "Dick Metzger knew some rather loathsome specimens. He introduced me to them." She paused again. "Wait— You weren't checking on *me*, Joseph Burke?"

He shook his head. "But thanks for the lead. I'll blackmail you into marrying me. How about the sport pages?"

She gave them to him and immersed herself in the drama page. He read that Cal had sewn up the Southern Division basketball title and Washington had cinched the Northern crown. The principals in a fight at the Olympic were being investigated. The fight had a bad odor. UCLA had won a soccer match from Stanford, one way to get around the spring football limitation. Indiana had the Big Ten basketball crown and was rated the best in the country by the U.P.

Norah asked, "Anything exciting in the world of sports, Mr. Burke?"

"Not much. How about the theatrical world?"

"That story Bruce Dysart was going to film has been turned down. So the poor author shouldn't have been so stubborn. He'd have had his money if he'd taken Bruce's offer."

"Somebody else will buy it, probably."

"But no other producer will give it the Dysart treatment. He played fair with everybody, according to Leonard. I guess, if Alan's really the heir, that should prove Leonard is right. Because Alan despised him, openly and vocally."

"That I'll give the kid—he's open and vocal."

"And sensitive and talented," Norah added.

"Maybe. He's bright enough. Or let me say he *sounds* bright enough. Some of these lippy boys sound brighter than they are."

"Yes, officer." Norah stood up. "It's too nice a day to work, but I'm going to. I need the money." She started to put the paper together and then stopped. "What's that? Did you hear that noise?"

"No. What kind of noise?"

"From the living-room. It sounded like someone knocking."

Joe rose and went into the living-room. A window was open there, and the shade was flapping against the frame. It wasn't a window he remembered opening.

He closed it as Norah came through from the kitchen.

"Thank heavens," she said. "I thought it might be Sharon again. Are you going to drive me to my car?"

"Of course. Norah, I don't remember opening that window."

"Stop it," she said. "I'm getting back to normal. What kind of prowler would prowl a policeman's house? Let's go."

Something came to Joe's mind and went away before he could identify it. He went to the bedroom to get the keys for his car.

He drove her to her car and then went over to Smith's house. Leonard was in front, spading a flower bed, digging in peat moss.

Joe asked, "Are we going to haul furniture today?"

Smith nodded. "I suppose. You look like you've swallowed a canary. What makes you so pleased with yourself this morning?"

"My money."

"I'll bet. Go get a couple cans of beer from the refrigerator, will you? I don't want to track up the house."

When Joe came back with the beer, Leonard was sitting on the bale of peat moss. Joe sat on the low porch.

Leonard looked uncomfortable. "I'm sorry about yesterday, Joe. It was—adolescent. I hate to see anybody being—casual about Norah."

"I asked her to marry me. How casual is that?"

Smith stared at him. "Well, that *is* different. And what did she say?"

"She said 'maybe.' Though not right now."

Smith smiled dimly. "I've still hope, then. I'll get some of those elevator shoes and wear a girdle and plaster my hair with perfumed pomade. I'll go down fighting."

The sun glinted off the beer cans. Across the street, a mailman was warily keeping an eye on a watching Doberman. Joe said nothing, feeling uncomfortable.

Smith chuckled. "I wasn't feeling sorry for myself. I was painting a picture of me for me."

"Tall girls don't seem to scare Mickey Rooney," Joe suggested. "You're not as short as you think you are, Leonard."

Smith smiled. "Thank you. I'll put this spade away and then we'll go and rent a trailer."

Smith had a list of the donors; they made the rounds. One of the items was a secretary, and they had a bad time with that. When they had finally maneuvered it onto the stage, Smith was breathing heavily.

He went over to sit on the davenport. "My doctor would scream if he saw me. I've a heart murmur, you know."

"You should have told me, Leonard. Somebody else could have helped with this."

"They all work for a living," Smith said. He looked around him. "Well, we've done our bit, haven't we? And it's going to look pretty good."

Joe nodded.

"A nothing," Smith went on. "All this work to put on a trite piece of Broadway corn without even the partial solace of being paid for it. Why?"

"That's what Alan Dysart wanted to know. He said there was artistic satisfaction in experimental theater but this kind of little theater was worse than TV."

"No. No wrestlers, no Skelton, no nauseating commercials; it's not worse than TV. But that's a weak comparison. It's still not worth the effort some of us put into it."

Joe laughed. "God, you're sour lately. Nobody's twisting your arm, Leonard. Get out of it."

Smith shook his head. "It's the only theater that will have me. I think I'll go home and take a nap."

Joe dropped him at home and then stopped off at the Point Realty Company. Norah was out, the office girl told him, showing a house.

He went home for lunch. After that a shower, and then he went out to the patio for some sun. Great life; no work, no worry, no time clock. Great life for a man of eighty.

He lay on the pad and stared at the foliage overhead through his sun glasses. He could travel, of course, but bored people usually carried their boredom with them. And he didn't like to travel alone.

With Norah, it would be fun traveling. Or with Sharon, for that matter. Or with any of a half dozen others he knew. But most fun with Norah. Yes, he had to have her, and not just in a bedroom. She would give some meaning to his days.

He thought back to his days in the Department, the foot-weary, corpse-filled routine of the later years in Homicide. What had he learned? He'd learned to play it safe, get along with the newspaper boys and not let his politics show. He'd learned not to talk back to his superiors and stay clear of controversial topics.

Hell, Alan was more of a man than he was in a lot of ways. Alan was loud and opinionated but at least he'd never learned to butter up to people who might help him. But then, he'd never had to learn. Somebody else had been paying his way. He could afford his opinions.

Larry Puma couldn't. So Larry polished the tired trivialities of past Broadway years, hoping the burnish would attract the eye of someone who could pay, pay, pay. . . .

And Sharon? That one he'd bank on. Who would ever stop that drive of hers, who could remain perpetually immune to the universal allure she projected? Sharon knew where she wanted to go and it wasn't too far for any single-minded person with her equipment. The surprise to Joe was the fact she hadn't made it by now.

From a bough of the eucalyptus tree at the back of his yard, a squirrel considered him brightly, its head cocked.

"Not yet," Joe said. "Another couple months of this and you can have me. But not yet."

The squirrel went around to the other side of the trunk and disappeared.

Joe heard the scrape of a foot and turned to see Krivick coming through the gate from the side yard. The sergeant looked tired.

He asked Joe, "Who were you talking to?"

"A squirrel. You look beat, Sergeant."

"Not enough to talk to squirrels. You wouldn't have a beer in the joint, would you?"

"Sit down, Sergeant. I'll get you one."

When he came back with a couple of cans, the sergeant was stretched out on the redwood chaise longue. "What a life you lead, you lucky dog."

"It's great. I've pretty sure information that Goetz is dead, Ernie."

"So have I. Where'd you get yours?"

"Just between us, from Ray Brennan. He saw him get on the plane."

"You went up against Brennan, without a badge? You have got guts, haven't you? Or is it your dough impressed him?"

"He owed me a favor, more or less."

Krivick took a deep pull at the beer. "That blonde, that Norah Payne, knew some of that kind of people, too. Including Dick Metzger."

"Metzger? Was he a criminal?"

"A pimp. Don't you remember him? Five-hundred-dollar call girls. Nobody ever nailed him, but I thought every cop in town knew what he was."

"My God!" Joe said. "I'm sure Norah Payne didn't know about him though, Ernie."

"Sure? How can you be sure? Have you known her long?"

"No. But I'm sure."

Krivick took another pull of his beer and wiped his mouth with the back of his hand. "Love. It must be love."

"Yup."

"No wonder you talk to squirrels. What a life. You lucky bastard." Krivick reached down to unlace his shoes and kick them off. "Strange you should mention Ray Brennan."

"Why?"

"Because his wife buys her shoes at Sam's Shoe Salon. She just happened to be in there today, when I walked in to talk to this Puma."

"A coincidence," Joe said.

"That you mentioned Brennan? Sure. But not that she buys her shoes at Sam's. Dames like her don't buy cheap shoes, and that's all Sam sells. And I'm sure she doesn't go in there to see Sam; he hasn't got that kind of a face."

"Maybe a pattern's starting to show, huh, Ernie?"

"Maybe. Though Goetz and Metzger aren't going to do

us much good where they are. And who's going to get rough with Ray Brennan's wife just because she buys cheap shoes? Not this cop."

"I'll get you another beer," Joe said.

When he came out again, Krivick's eyes were closed and his breathing was heavy and regular. Joe went in again and brought out a blanket. He covered Krivick carefully so as not to awaken him.

Then his phone rang and he went in once more. It was the pigeon named Arty. He said, "Goetz is dead, all right, Joe. I got it right from the horse's mouth."

"Thanks, Arty. Drop over tomorrow and I'll have the hundred for you. It's the gospel, eh?"

"Got it right from the widow," Arty told him. "She never married again, though she's been set up here and there. Anything you want at Santa Anita, Joe?"

"Not this week. The widow wouldn't lie about it, would she?"

"I doubt it like hell. But who can be real sure about women? Right, Joe? Except for Vera, of course. But there aren't many like Vera. Right?"

"Right," Joe said. And after he'd hung up: "Thank God."

CHAPTER NINE

THE SUN was below the rear wall of the patio now, and it was cool. From the redwood chaise longue came the soft sound of Krivick's snoring.

Joe went into the kitchen and started to prepare dinner. *Five-hundred-dollar call girls. . . . Had Norah known? Had Norah. . . .* He stopped that thought half-born.

He snapped on the small kitchen radio to the news. From the neighborhood came the sounds of returning cars, of slamming garage doors. In the kitchen, the refrigerator hummed and the small radio was warning citrus growers about the possibility of frost in Pomona.

Krivick came into the kitchen, the blanket over his arm. "You shouldn't have let me sleep, Joe."

"Relax, Ernie. Get a beer from the refrigerator. I'm fixing you a porterhouse."

Krivick paused to look at it. "I'll phone the wife."

"Do that. Do you like Roquefort dressing on your salad?"

"Hell, yes. Where'd you learn to cook, Joe?"

"On twelve years of Department pay, could I eat out? I had to learn."

"How come you never married, Joe? You ain't queer, I hope?"

"Queer enough to know two can't live on what I made. I'm going to get married now. I can afford it."

Krivick shook his head. "Now you can afford not to

be married. Well, I'll call the wife."

Over their pre-dinner cans of beer, Joe said, "We open the show tonight. Maybe, if you hung around, you'd learn something."

"Maybe. I've got a feeling this is one of those merry-go-rounds where everybody looks guilty and nobody gets indicted. But I've been lucky on the last three; that should carry me through a flop."

"This one's big, though, Ernie."

"You're telling me? Don't remind me."

Joe laughed, and stopped laughing at Krivick's stricken look.

The steak was juicy and flavorful, the salad fine. Joe had made garlic bread and Krivick ate most of that. As Joe poured the coffee, Krivick leaned back and loosened his belt. "That was some meal, Joe. What a life."

"You wouldn't trade it for your three daughters, would you?"

Krivick grinned. "Hell, no. God, that youngest one's going to be a beauty. And bright! No, Joe, I wouldn't trade you."

They did the dishes together, and it was only a little after seven. But Joe said, "Maybe they'll need some help to set up the chairs. We'd better go now."

There were two hundred chairs set up when they got there, and that should have been more than enough. A paid attendance of a hundred was an exceptional opening night. Tonight the two hundred chairs were filled an hour before curtain time.

Norah was there to handle the lights and she helped Joe and Pete Delahunt set up more chairs. Krivick got into the spirit of it, as the customers continued to pour in, and Krivick hauled the additional chairs from the shed behind the clubhouse.

"Ghouls," Norah said. "But they're all paying. Maybe some of them will like the play enough to come again."

"We live in hope," Pete Delahunt agreed. He turned to Joe. "That sergeant's a pretty good guy, isn't he?"

Joe nodded.

"I suppose he's working, though?" Pete said. "This isn't a social call."

Joe nodded again. "He's always working." Then he looked past Pete toward the doorway. Krivick was standing there, talking to a man and a woman.

Joe didn't recognize the woman. But the man was Ray Brennan.

There was a total paid attendance of four hundred and ninety, a new opening night record.

Krivick came over to sit next to Joe in the last row of chairs along the back wall. Joe asked him, "Is that Brennan's wife with him?"

"That's her. Maybe she came to see Puma, eh?"

"Or maybe it was Brennan's idea," Joe suggested, "though I didn't mention anything to him but Lonnie Goetz."

"He can read," Krivick said, "and your name's been in the paper in connection with this murder. Hey, look at that."

Two rows ahead of them, Larry Puma was sitting down next to Mrs. Brennan. Ray leaned over to welcome him as he sat down.

And then the lights were dimmed, and the curtain was going up.

Joe had seen it in fits and starts and pieces; this was his first view of it as a unified, dramatic whole. Larry had given it all the meaning the author had written into it—and more. It moved, it sparkled, it made sense.

As the lights went on, at the end of the first act, Krivick said, "This is almost as good as *Boston Blackie*. This bunch is okay, right?"

"Right, Ernie. How about some coffee and a doughnut? I'll buy."

Out in the patio, they were joined by Norah and Larry Puma. Then Krivick asked Puma, "Would you come around the corner here for a minute? I've a few questions."

As they walked around the end of the building with their coffee and doughnuts, Joe noticed Brennan watching them from in front of the counter. Then Brennan's roving glance came to Joe, and he waved.

Norah said, "Who's the man with white hair?"

"His name is Brennan. He's a former narcotics king."

"You do have the nicest friends."

Joe thought of Dick Metzger. He said nothing.

"And why," Norah went on, "does your friend want to talk to Larry Puma?"

"I don't know, honey. The play's going all right, isn't it?"

"Beautifully. Here comes your white-haired friend and his girl." Norah lighted a cigarette. "He certainly doesn't look like a—a criminal."

Brennan introduced Joe to his wife, and then Joe introduced both of them to Norah. Mrs. Brennan was a brunette, thirty years her husband's junior. She was a pretty woman and pleasant enough.

As the warning lights flashed for the second act, Ray said, "Would you wait a moment, Joe? I'd like a few words in private."

After the others had gone back in, Brennan said quietly, "That question you asked me yesterday, did it have something to do with what happened here a few nights ago?"

Joe hesitated and then nodded. "One of the suspects in the case used to know Lonnie."

Brennan smiled. "Mmmm-hmmm. She used to live with him. I recognized her as soon as I saw her up on that stage. What's she doing in a fly-blown outfit like this?"

Joe shrugged. "What's Larry Puma doing here? He has plenty on the ball, too."

"That's what my wife's been trying to tell me. Chloe

used to be in the theater. If burlesque is theater. I had a feeling, at first, this Puma was back-dooring me. But I guess he's on the level. What do you think, Joe?"

"I like him, though I don't know him very well. I just joined this group a week ago."

"Joined? Is that why you're messing in this murder? You belong to this gang?"

Joe nodded. "Why else would I be here? I left the Department when I inherited that money."

Brennan finished the last of his coffee and set the cup on one of the Ping-pong tables. "I see, I see. I'd never played pigeon before, Joe, and it worried me. And then after you'd left, I realized there might be a possibility Lonnie was alive. I saw him go up the ramp to the plane, sure. But when there wasn't any insurance, and—well, I knew there was a very remote possibility he could have come down from the plane again, after I stopped looking. I mean, if he is alive, I want to know it. Do you know, Joe?"

"I don't know. There was a rumor that he was alive and in town. His widow claims he's dead, and the first rumor might not have been reliable."

"A stoolie?"

"Could be. I don't know."

Brennan took a deep pull of his cigarette and dropped it to the concrete. "Well, Chloe will be wondering where I am. That redhead, that Sharon, sure reaches out across those lights, doesn't she?"

"She's got it," Joe agreed. "She's come a long way from Lonnie Goetz."

Brennan smiled. "I wouldn't say that. Lonnie was never tight with his women and this Sharon can't be making much here. Stay sober, Joe." He patted Joe's arm and walked off toward the door to the auditorium.

Larry Puma was picking up the discarded paper cups and putting them into a garbage can. Joe went over to help him.

Larry looked puzzled. "Was that true what the sergeant told me? Is Chloe's husband a racketeer?"

"Not any more. He's retired. He used to be the big man in the local narcotics trade. Is it true what Brennan told me, that Chloe was in burlesque?"

"For two months. Did he also mention she'd worked with the Lunts for two years?"

"No."

"He wouldn't. Why Chloe should marry that bag of bones is beyond me."

Joe laughed. "Not too far beyond you, I hope. Have you ever been up to his house?"

"Yes. Once. A party. That still doesn't answer my question. There are wealthy, *decent* men, too, you know."

"And plenty of willing women to snag them. Larry, I never thought I'd have to tell you to grow up."

Larry dumped a handful of discarded napkins into the can. Joe brought over the soiled paper spoons he'd collected. From the auditorium, a murmur of laughter ran through the audience.

Puma began to collect the sugar bowls. "I think I've had enough of this. Is that what you meant by growing up?"

"You know it isn't. I meant facing certain realities, and one of them is that women appreciate security."

"*Appreciate* it? They worship it. It's their god. So the men scramble and scratch and cut each other's throats. Is that natural for men?"

"I guess not, Larry. You're bitter tonight."

"Sure. I worked on this play. I brought out qualities in it even the author didn't intend. It's a piece of fluff, but I'm proud of the job I did on it, if you'll pardon the immodesty."

"I'll pardon it. What's your point?"

"Only this—what comes across, what projects most vividly of all?"

"You tell me."

"Sharon. Her red hair and her fine bust and that throaty, phony, burlesque huskiness of hers. That's what the audience gets. *This* audience, at least. I've been watching them, and she's *it*, to them."

Joe wanted to smile, but he didn't. He said, "And then your Chloe with that bag of bones and Krivick dragging you around the corner like a thief. This has been a bad night for you, Larry. Tomorrow will be better."

Larry looked at him scornfully. "Cut out the Pollyanna crap, will you? Tomorrow we work until nine o'clock at Sam's Shoe Salon. Tomorrow I sit at the feet of women for eleven hours."

Joe brought the sugar bowls and cream pitchers to the counter for refilling. Walter Hamilton's wife, Jean, smiled at him. "Thank you. Larry in another of his moods?"

"He's in a mood. Does this happen often?"

"No oftener than it does to any of us. Larry's more vocal." She began to rinse out the cream pitchers. "And more talented, which makes it worse, I suppose."

"Does it happen to Walter?"

She sighed. "Only rarely. Walter's older and more— adjusted."

"I suppose," Joe said, "a playhouse of their own would make them all happy."

She was pouring sugar. "It would help." She looked up quickly. "Joe Burke, you weren't thinking of— You—" She stared at him, out of words.

"Just this second, and only for a second. Forget I mentioned it."

She nodded, studying him. "You used the word 'playhouse.' Did you say that instead of 'theater' for a reason? Children, playing games—was that your thought?"

"Not consciously. There's nothing wrong with children playing games, is there? I like the picture. Jean, if you tell Walter I made that slip about your own theater, I'll—"

She smiled at him. "Yes, *officer*. It's our secret." She blew him a kiss.

Larry had gone back into the auditorium; Joe went in to find his chair next to Krivick again.

Krivick whispered, "Say, you know, this is all right. I figured, with amateurs and all, you know, it would be corny, but—"

From the row ahead, a lady turned to glare at them. From the other end of their row, someone said, "Ssshhh!"

Krivick nudged Joe. "Commies. I'll have McCarthy investigate 'em."

The second act went on smoothly, the Puma touch evident in every line and gesture and piece of business. But it was in Sharon's scenes that the silence was most nearly absolute, the audience reaction most nearly immediate.

The second act curtain went down to a solid wall of applause.

"That redhead," Krivick said, "what a dish." He stood up. "Let's go out and have a cigarette."

In the patio, Pete Delahunt joined them. He was looking happy. "I can guess why they came, but some of them are going to come back. What a job Larry's done on this turkey."

"Fine," Joe agreed. He looked over toward the doorway where Larry and the Brennans were pleasantly chatting.

Krivick said, "If you ask me, that redhead's carrying the whole show."

Pete Delahunt looked pained. Joe said, "I'm glad I didn't ask you, Ernie."

"So I'm out of order," Krivick said. "I ain't had your long experience in the theater, Mr. Burke. I'll buy the coffee." He went over to the counter.

Delahunt asked, "Anything new on the—" He stopped. "Nothing much."

Delahunt was watching Krivick at the counter. "Alan

Dysart moved into his uncle's house today. So he must be the heir. I didn't see anything in the paper about it, though."

"Dysart's attorneys aren't the kind that need cheap publicity, probably."

Krivick came with the paper cups full of coffee. "You guys want doughnuts, too?"

Joe shook his head. Pete asked, "Does this mean I'm in the clear, Sergeant? You wouldn't buy coffee for a killer, would you?"

Krivick smiled. "You're as clear as anybody, I guess. Especially since you're scared of firearms."

Pete stared at the sergeant. "How'd you know that?"

Krivick didn't answer.

Joe laughed. "What do you think cops do with their time, Pete? They work, work, *work*."

"So they work. But there were *two* people in the world who knew that about me."

"And now there are three," Joe said. "Four, with me. Ernie isn't much of a dramatic critic, but he knows his trade. He's no amateur."

"Keep talking," Krivick said. "I can use the publicity."

The warning lights went on and off and on; they went in for the third act.

The illusion was constant, the magic continued. A shoe clerk's polish on a hack's bit of nothing given meaning by part-time players under the shadow of the basketball backboard.

A small glimmer in a dark night. Joe fingered the bandage on his skull, proud of his seven stitches.

Six curtain calls and then some of the audience headed for the doors; the others went up to the stage to congratulate the players.

Norah came out from the light booth and headed their way.

Krivick said, "This blonde coming over; that's for you,

huh, Joe?"

"If she'll have me."

"With your dough? Well, I'd better be getting home. The missus will be waiting. Thanks for the meal and the show and the beer, Joe."

"You're welcome. If I learn anything interesting, I'll get in touch with you, Ernie."

"Do that." Krivick nodded at Norah, coming up, and went past her, toward the door.

Norah said, "It came off, didn't it? It played beautifully."

"It did to me. I'm no judge."

"For a turkey like this, you're an excellent judge. Wasn't it great? Aren't you excited? Where's Larry?"

"It was great. I'm not excited. Larry's talking to the white-haired man and his wife, over there near the door."

"Oh, that Brennan person. *She's* nice, though, isn't she?"

"Two years with the Lunts," Joe said. "And two months in burlesque. Larry thinks she's special."

"Well, then, she is. Larry's bright about people. We ought to have a party, Joe. Wouldn't you like a party?"

"I've a house full of liquor," Joe agreed. "You invite the people you want. But not Ray Brennan. I don't want him in my house."

"All right. I'll invite all the people I want. And Sharon, too. She does register, doesn't she, Joe? She does project."

Joe lied with a shrug. "I've seen too many of the type."

Norah put a hand on his lips. "That was nice. I'll go ask the gang."

It came off better than his Department party. Pete Delahunt brought mix from the local liquor store and Smith picked up a carful of chop suey from the Chinese restaurant.

They danced, they gabbed, they drank and ate and

argued and laughed and forgot the time clock waiting for them.

Norah said, "Actors make fine parties. I suppose because parties are an illusion, too."

"I'm trying to follow you," Joe said, "but I've had a lot of whisky."

"I mean parties are pretending we're gay and bright and adventurous, even though we're not really any of those things." She moved close to him. "Dance with me again. Where did you learn to dance?"

"At the Palladium. Where did you?"

"At dancing school. Why is it that people learn it better at public dance halls?"

"They give it more time. I used to dance three nights a week."

"You must know lots of girls."

"Too many."

"Weren't you ever in love, Joe?"

"Not since I left high school. Not until a few days ago."

She looked up at him, and he kissed her, and next to them Pete Delahunt said, "None of that." He was dancing with Jean Hamilton, and Jean held a small clenched fist aloft in approbation.

Then Leonard Smith cut in, saying, "I'm just drunk enough not to give a damn about my height. Let's give it a whirl, Norah."

Joe grinned at both of them and went out into the kitchen. Sharon was in there, sitting in the breakfast nook with Walter.

Hamilton said, "Fine liquor you serve, sir. Is my wife behaving?"

"She's dancing with Pete." Joe mixed himself a drink and brought it over to the nook. He slid in next to Walter. "Having a good time?"

"With this kind of whisky? Who wouldn't?" Walter looked at Sharon. "But our ingénue seems to be sulking."

"Nobody in there misses me, I'm sure," Sharon said. "Who were those people Larry was talking to at the play, Joe?"

"Mr. and Mrs. Ray Brennan."

Sharon nodded. "I thought I remembered him. Are they friends of Larry's?"

"I guess."

Sharon smiled. "That should be interesting to Sergeant Krivick."

Joe said nothing. Walter asked, "Am I missing something I should be getting?"

Sharon patted Walter's hand. "Nothing. Why don't we dance?"

Hamilton slid out. "It will be an honor and a pleasure, at least for me."

They went out through the doorway to the dining-room.

A few seconds later, Larry and Norah came through from the entrance hall. Larry was a little unsteady on his feet.

He said, "Behold the sulking host. Fine whisky, Joe."

"My feet wouldn't take any more of it," Norah said. "I brought him in here. Why aren't you mixing with your guests, sir?"

Larry slid in next to Joe; Norah sat across from them. Joe said, "I was mixing with my guests. They just went in to dance. How are you feeling, Lady Norah?"

"Fine. But I think Larry's close to the edge. Aren't you, Larry?"

Larry waved a hand. "Don't worry about me. I never get obnoxious. I simply go to sleep." He put a flat hand on the table top. "And dream of Sam's Shoe Salon."

Joe said quietly, "I was thinking of a bigger dream for all of you."

Both of them looked at him wonderingly.

Joe looked at Larry. "A theater of your own, that house

you've been dreaming of. And a little more. I'd have it converted for you. You'd want a real lighting system with a first-rate switchboard. And a stage you could splash in."

Larry was suddenly un-drunk. "God, Joe, don't take advantage of my drunkenness. This is no gag?"

Joe shook his head. "I'd want you in charge of it, Larry. No salary, but if you could live on what you pulled out of it, you're welcome to any profit."

Larry's fists were clenched now on top of the table. "I've eaten on four dollars a week, and I can do it again. I don't understand why you want me, though, Joe."

"Because I think you can get along with people at all levels. That much, Sam must have taught you. Here's a condition of it: there must be room for Alan Dysart and others of that school."

Both Norah and Larry looked puzzled.

Joe said, "I think this Dysart has something to say, if he'd stop talking and start working. I think all the bright ones have. But I don't want this purely experimental. Because it should be a training ground and some actors are never going to be trained beyond the kind of nothing we put on tonight. I figure you've got more balance than anybody else in the group." Joe smiled. "So there."

Larry killed a belch, half-born. "What a bomb to throw at me in this condition. About Alan, Joe; I can get along with him. I can get along with anybody. But could he get along with us? He isn't the kind who'd stand still for *Abie's Irish Rose*. And he's got enough money now for a theater of his own."

"He was just a symbol," Joe said. "There'll be other Alans. It was a point I was trying to make."

"Oh." Larry smiled. "You must have talked to him and he drowned you in words you didn't understand. Let me say quite frankly and without malice, Joe, they were words he didn't understand, either. But he can read and he can dream. He's another Dick Metzger."

Norah said, "What a rotten remark! You always resented Dick, didn't you?" She sat rigidly on the bench.

Larry shook his head. "I felt kind of sorry for him. Until I learned he was a pimp. Grow up, Norah."

Joe stopped Norah's clenched hand before it reached Larry's face. He stayed there, leaning over the table, while he took her other hand. "Larry wasn't lying. Dick Metzger dealt in expensive call girls, and the police knew it."

Norah was the color of bleached bone. Her gaze moved bleakly over Joe's face. "You knew it, and didn't tell me?"

"Why not? He's dead, isn't he? Whatever he was doesn't matter now. *He's dead*. Why should I make you unhappy? I love you too much for that."

She was still rigid on the bench but her hands gripped Joe's tightly and tears moved down her cheeks.

Larry put both open hands to his face. "I'd better be getting home. Big day at the store tomorrow."

Joe said, "You're in no shape to drive, Larry. Better stay here. And you might as well say good-by to the store now, if you're accepting my offer. You might as well leave Sam tonight."

Larry slid out and stood up. "I'll sleep here, but set an alarm, will you? I wouldn't do that to Sam, not on a big day. I owe Sam plenty."

Joe grinned. "I'm glad you said that. It's the kind of talk I can understand. I'll show you your room."

When he came back to the kitchen, Norah was drinking a cup of coffee.

"That's stale," Joe told her. "I could have made some fresh coffee."

"It doesn't matter. I want to get home, Joe, and get some sleep. It's after two."

"Stay here if you want. We're chaperoned."

She shook her head. "I've some things to do in the morning, some things to—dispose of."

He sat across from her. "I'm sorry. I'm truly sorry."

She faced him candidly. "I'm not. Burning incense is no work for a red-blooded American girl." She reached over and took his head in both her hands and kissed him.

From the doorway to the dining-room, Pete Delahunt said, "Is that all you two do? What kind of house is this?"

"*Our* house," Norah answered. "We're going to be married."

The last guest had gone and the smell of cigarette smoke was heavy in all the rooms they'd used. Joe went around opening windows and picking up glasses. The glasses he stacked on the drainboard of the sink. He emptied the ash trays into the garbage grinder. Then he poured himself another cup of coffee and sat in the nook.

It had been some day. It seemed like a week ago that he had stood next to his bed looking down at Norah. But that had opened this day.

Or rather, this yesterday. For it was almost four o'clock.

It had been a full day and a revealing one. It had been a long day and his eyes were getting heavy. He thought of the theater he planned to give them and the thought was warming. His small sound.

He had set the alarm in the room Larry occupied; he went to bed without setting his own.

He didn't open his eyes until nearly eleven o'clock. He lay a while, stretching, and then went out to put water on to boil.

By the time he'd finished shaving, the water was boiling and he measured the coffee into the basket. He set the timer and went in to see if Larry had got up in time. He must have; the room was empty.

His front doorbell rang and he went to find Arty the pigeon standing there.

"Damn it," Joe said, "I forgot all about going to the bank yesterday, Arty. A check do it?"

"Why not?"

"Come on in. I'm just making breakfast. Could I fix you a couple of eggs?"

Arty came in and looked around. "Some joint." He followed Joe to the kitchen. "Nothing to eat, but I could use a cup of coffee. Boy, you hit it, huh, Joe?"

"I hit it." Joe nodded toward the breakfast-nook table. "What's new on this Dysart kill?"

"Nothing." Joe poured him a cup of coffee. "Do you hear anything about it?"

Arty shrugged and sat at the table. "Nothing solid. There's a persistent rumor it could have been political. But not from any sources I give a second thought to. You know, bar talk." He poured a good helping of cream into his coffee and stirred it thoughtfully. "I did hear you went up against Ray Brennan."

"You've got big ears, Arty. I'll get my checkbook."

He was going to the bedroom when his phone rang.

It was Krivick. "Busy?"

"Nope."

"Would you come over to Dysart's? You know the house?"

"I know it. What's happened?"

"Alan Dysart's been murdered."

CHAPTER TEN

THERE WERE TWO DEPARTMENT CARS in front of the Dysart house when Joe got there. Neighbors all around were out on their lawns and a knot of kids stood on the sidewalk in front of the house.

To the uniformed man at the door Joe said, "Sergeant Krivick sent for me. I'm Joe Burke."

The man nodded and gestured toward an open, curved staircase. "He's up in the bedroom."

In a huge bedroom the width of the house near the top of the stairs, Krivick stood near a window overlooking the street. One of the technical boys was working with silver nitrate on some water tumblers on the double dresser.

Krivick turned and stared bleakly at Joe. "Ain't this just dandy?"

"How long has he been dead, Ernie?"

"Don't know for sure, but it must be five or six hours. He's stiff."

"How was he killed?"

"Shot through the eye." Krivick took a breath. "With a .32."

Joe looked toward the bed. There was only a mound under the silk comforter; Alan's face was covered.

Krivick said, "Won't the heat be on now! What the hell is it, an epidemic?"

Joe said, "I just thought of something. Alan was nosing into his uncle's death."

Krivick's glare was bitter. "*Now* you thought of it.

When'd you learn that?"

"The other day. Smith told me he saw him rummaging through that incinerator at the playground. I asked Alan about it and he said he was looking for the gun, that that seemed a logical place to dispose of it."

"An amateur Hawkshaw." Krivick shook his head. "There's another angle. Something could have been stolen. Come on down to the study."

The study was behind the living-room and a step lower. It was as wide as the living-room, paneled in Philippine mahogany, its entire west wall of glass, overlooking the patio and rear yard.

Krivick led Joe directly to a desk and pulled out one of the drawers. From the front it had looked like three drawers, but it was actually one.

It held a wire recorder.

Krivick said, "Someone who didn't know how to do it right took a spool off of there and ruined the spindle. Like a person would who meant to get the spool in a hurry and who didn't give a damn about the machine."

Joe frowned. "Sounds kind of phony to me, Ernie."

"Sure, sure. But this was a phony guy, this young Dysart. See the microphone here, hidden in this lamp? Right out of a B picture. How phony can you get?"

"I'm not following you, Ernie."

"Well, first of all, he was investigating the murder, wasn't he?"

"Maybe. He was looking through that incinerator."

"Okay. Just a theory, then. The killer was here, say this afternoon. At Dysart's request. The kid accuses him, taking the conversation down. Maybe the killer admits it, maybe not. But the kid's accusations are here, on the wire. If the killer learned that, wouldn't he come back?"

Joe studied the spindle. "Anybody with any sense would see in a second how to take that spool off without wrecking the spindle. You're really reaching, Ernie."

"Maybe. I'm trying to locate one of Bruce Dysart's former servants now. I'll find out if Bruce wired that recorder that way, or if it was done since the kid moved in."

Joe asked, "Why do you figure there's a lapse of time between this theoretical accusation and the kill?"

"The kid was killed in bed, in his pajamas. It doesn't figure he'd accuse the killer and then go to bed while he was still in the house."

Joe shook his head. "*If* there's been an accusation. Anyone in the neighborhood hear the shot?"

"I've got men out checking on that now. There's something else missing, Joe." He went over to push back a sliding door and reveal a wall of shelves. Cans of film were stacked solid here, except for a gap on the second row. The gap was just wide enough for one can.

"Take a look at this dust on the edge of the second shelf," Krivick said.

There was a clean spot on the shelf where one of the heavy cans had obviously been dragged out.

Krivick said, "That's been done since Bruce Dysart's death."

"Maybe Alan took it out."

"A good guess. But where is it *now?*"

Joe shrugged and went back to the wire recorder. "Kid stuff, right out of a private-eye movie. I can see him sitting here, Ernie, matching his superior brain against the killer's solving this simple murder for the dumb cops. Big hero."

"Dead hero. You beginning to believe my way, Joe?"

"I said I could picture it. It makes a good picture. But you don't take mental pictures into court. If the kid sat here, *who* sat on the other side of the desk?"

"Whoever's got that can and that spool of wire. They aren't so easy to get rid of. You can't just dump 'em; they have to be destroyed. Or hidden."

"Film would be easy to destroy. And to destroy what's

on that wire, you could run it on another player. The new sound erases the old."

"Does the killer know that? A killer who doesn't even know how to take off the spool?"

"An amateur killer," Joe added, "who probably used the same gun twice. Can you check that?"

"I don't think so. This slug's all right. Went into the pillow. But that first one was battered. I'll get a report from ballistics when I go back to the station. If you wanted to get rid of that wire, what would you do, Joe?"

"I'd take it off the spool and put it in an empty, closed coffee can. I'd drive to where there was a can collection and dump it in some citizen's box."

"Would you? No. Somebody could be watching, and wouldn't they wonder about a stranger adding a can to their collection? And the can the film was in, how about that?"

"Once the film is burned, the can can be dumped any-where."

"Unless it's labeled. And labeled with a metal tag, riveted on, as a lot of these are."

Joe said nothing. Ernie looked too hopeful. It wasn't a time to remind him how big this town was, and how many hiding places it held. Or how easily that metal tag could be removed.

Krivick said, "Maybe this second killing is a break. For everybody but young Dysart and the killer."

"I hope so," Joe told him. "Most of the gang were at my house last night, Ernie. I threw a party."

"You figure out when they left, as best you can, huh? The ones you don't know about, ask somebody else. Would you do that for me, Joe?"

"I'd be glad to, Ernie. I'll do more than that, if you want: some unofficial investigating. If I stick my neck out, would you back me up?"

Krivick nodded. "But if you've an idea on it, I'm listening, Joe."

"If I had an idea, I'd tell you. See you, Ernie."

Joe didn't go down to his car immediately; he walked the fifty feet to the entrance to the playground tennis courts at the bottom of the slope. There was another, smaller parking area down here, probably for the use of the tennis players.

From Dysart's house a person could walk to the club-house without being in view of any of the homes after the first fifty feet of the trip. The road was below the level of the lots around it and all the rear yards were surrounded by high fences.

He was just getting into his car when Leonard Smith came along the sidewalk.

Leonard looked haggard. "What's all the rumpus at Dysart's?"

"Alan's dead."

Smith stared at him quietly.

"Murdered," Joe added.

Smith looked past Joe, at the Dysart home. "God— Who can it be, Joe?"

"I don't know."

The round face of Leonard Smith seemed gray and dead. "Alan—" He shook his head. "Oh, God— The man had so much—oh, fire and dedication. He was such an uncompromising punk, it was refreshing to know there were young people with— I don't know what the hell I'm saying." He stared at Joe. "I must be off my nut. The arguments I've had with that kid, and now it's like I've lost a son."

Joe nodded. "Maybe his uncle felt that way about him, too."

"He did," Smith said. "I'm sure he did. If Alan had ever steadied down to the groove he was destined for, he— Well, what the hell difference does it make? He's dead."

"Simmer down, Leonard. You look sick."

"I am."

Joe hesitated and then said, "I wonder if you remember what time the various guests left my party last night?"

"I don't even remember what time I left. Joe, do the police think one of us is the—" He broke off.

"They think of the possibility," Joe answered quietly. "Leonard, what's the matter?" He put a hand on Smith's shoulder.

Smith's eyes were closed and he seemed to waver on his feet. He reached out and took hold of Joe's arm. "A little heart flutter. Nothing to get panicky about"—he opened his eyes—"I like to believe. I guess it was the shock, a delayed reaction."

Something flickered in Joe's mind and went away. It was the same kind of mind murmur he'd had when he'd found the open window in his living-room. But nothing definite came through to his conscious mind.

He asked, "Want to sit in the car for a minute, Leonard?"

Smith shook his head. "I'm all right now. It was only that Alan wasn't the sort of person I can picture as dead. He was so alive, so—aware."

"I know." Joe climbed into his car. "I'll be seeing you, Leonard. Take it easy."

Driving off, he reflected that the advice was unnecessary; Leonard had been taking it easy for quite a while.

At the Point Realty Company the office girl informed Joe that Norah hadn't come in yet but was expected any minute.

Joe drove out Sunset toward her apartment. Ahead of him a huge truck was picking up the cans; receptacles lined the street all the way to the bend at Marquez.

These were mostly apartment buildings along here and Krivick was wrong in thinking the addition of one can would invoke neighborhood interest. Especially if a person picked the collection in front of one of the larger buildings. What apartment dweller was familiar with all his neighbors?

Norah's car was at the curb. Joe parked behind it and went along the walk that led to the rear apartments. The building was constructed in a narrow U. Norah was on the second-floor balcony, drying her hair.

"Hide the bleach," Joe called out. "I'm coming up."

She made a face at him. "You would. No make-up on and my hair all over the place."

He came up the wooden steps that led to the balcony and stopped at her open door for a moment to peer in. "Cozy place you have."

She smiled at him, running a comb through her fine, bright hair. "I'm thinking of moving to a big place overlooking the ocean. Kiss me."

He leaned over to kiss her, and then moved a box of curlers from a low redwood bench so he could sit down. "I've bad news, Norah."

She stopped combing to look at him anxiously.

He said quietly, "Alan Dysart's dead."

She sat there, staring at him, the comb still poised in one upraised hand. "Joe—no— How, Joe? How did he die?"

"He was shot. Murdered."

"Oh, God—" She set the comb on the bench. "Alan. And *now*, now that he could finally do what he wanted. Oh, it can't be, Joe."

"It is." He pulled out a package of cigarettes and offered her one.

Her hand shook as he held a light for her. She said weakly, "What kind of a monster is this? Is there any reason, any *sane* reason why—" She stopped and looked fixedly at the floor of the balcony. "I'm getting sick."

Joe rose and went to her little kitchenette. When he came back with a glass of water, her face was paper-white. He held the glass while she sipped.

She drank about half the water and smiled weakly at

him. "After—last night's revelation and then this. God, Joe, what kind of world do we live in?"

"You could ask any cop. Or mission worker. Or Hollywood agent. I'm naïve, remember?"

She put a hand on his. "You're my rock. Why don't we get married and take a trip, a trip to some place where there aren't any *people?*"

He turned her hand over and held it in both of his. "This is our world. We're people."

"Not that kind. I haven't your hardness, Joe. I'm too much of a sissy. Maybe I should have gone to Cedar Rapids that time."

"I'm glad you didn't. Well, there are some people I have to see." He rose. "They're expecting you at the office."

"To hell with them; I'm marrying money." She looked up at him gravely. "Do you think it's your money I'm marrying?"

"I don't think so. It doesn't matter much; you're enough of a lady to make it a complete marriage anyway. And I'm enough of a Republican to be glad I'm rich. So we'll be happy."

He flicked her nose with a forefinger and went down the steps to the court.

She was leaning over the railing now. "Hey, when am I going to see you again?"

"I'll be at the play. I'm going to work on this last kill, Norah. I'll be busy most of the day."

She waved. "Good hunting, darling. Be careful."

He blew her a kiss.

The can truck hadn't arrived here yet. And the collection box was out of the range of Norah's vision. Joe went over to check through one of the larger ones, conscious of the absurdity of it but following a dim and impelling hunch.

It was a large box and he was halfway through it when a voice above him said, "If you're that hungry, I'll lend you a buck."

From the top of the truck a huge Negro grinned down at him.

"I was looking for a diamond ring," Joe said. "My wife left it in one of the coffee cans." He shrugged. "Oh, well, it was only five carats."

The Negro nodded. "And no peas? Are you through, mister?"

From the cab the driver said, "Let's go, Dean; we're behind now."

Joe could hear them laughing as he walked to his car.

It was a sunny day again, a return to the ridiculous weather. Joe took Sunset to Bundy and Bundy to Santa Monica Boulevard. At Doheny, he cut up the hill, back to Sunset.

The office building on Selma and Ivar was a three-story stucco place, full of winding halls and small offices. On the first floor, a reading-fee literary racketeer had taken over everything but the broom closet.

On the second floor, Nels Nystrom was dozing behind the desk in his dusty office. He opened his eyes and nodded at Joe.

"Business can't be that bad," Joe said. He sat in the worn, tapestry-covered pull-up chair on the customer's side of the desk.

Nels yawned and picked a half-smoked cigar from the rim of an ash tray on his desk. He examined it. "Krivick's been here. Is it the same kill that brings you here, Joe?"

"I left the Department months ago."

"I know." Nystrom's broad face was sadly patient. "Once a cop, always a cop."

"You were a cop, too, Nels."

Nystrom was lighting the cigar with a wooden match. "Is it about Bruce Dysart, Joe? Or Alan?"

"It was Bruce I wanted to talk to you about. I've money, now, Nels."

Nystrom rubbed sleepily at the back of his fat neck. "Did you plan to hire me with some of it?"

"I'll pay for what I can get. You worked for Bruce Dysart, didn't you, back in the days when you worked?"

Nystrom nodded. "When he was smoking out the Lenin-lovers. I even bought a beret and joined the Screen Writers' Guild. I had to work on one of his pictures to be eligible, but that wasn't hard; my daughter wrote the whole script for me. She was almost in high school then, and bright. How much is that worth, Joe?"

"I can get that out of the *Times* morgue."

"Why didn't you?"

"Because I thought for money you might tell me more."

"That's all there is, Joe, except for the Radio Writers' Guild. My daughter couldn't help me with that; her stuff was too subtle. You see, she was in high school by then and—"

"If I want a comedian," Joe interrupted, "I can tune in Jackie Gleason. Dysart liked your work, didn't he?"

"He said he did." The pudgy man sat a little straighter in his chair. "Why shouldn't he?"

"There's no reason he shouldn't," Joe said casually. "I thought that if he was satisfied with your work, he'd hire you for any other business he might have."

Nystrom wasn't sleepy now. "Have you a point to make or are you fishing, Joe?"

"I'm fishing. Did you do anything besides the Guild work for him?"

"Nothing you'd be interested in hearing about, nothing that would tie up with the murder. Or murders."

Joe took a deep breath. "You haven't anything to sell me; is that what you're saying, Nels?"

"That's it. Unless you're looking for a 1947 Plymouth?"

Joe stood up. "I'm not. But I should think a man driving a car that old would be more interested in money than you are." He lighted a cigarette. "Well, if you change your mind, phone me, Nels. Want my number?"

Nystrom shook his head.

Joe studied him. "Aren't you scared?"

Nystrom frowned. "What do you mean?"

"If you know anything, you should be scared. Alan learned something and got a bullet in the face. I hope you're being careful."

Nystrom chuckled. "Any second now, I expect to see a man come through the door behind you wearing a tight trench coat and a sneer. Aren't you being kind of theatrical, Joe?"

"I hope so. I hope you know what you're doing, Nels. The Department doesn't love you too much, anyway, you know. You should have some friends."

Nystrom stared at him blandly. "Good-by, Joe. Drop in again next year."

"If you're still here. If you're alive." Joe went out.

Only two things could overrule the lure of money in Nystrom's mind—fear of reprisal or more money. Though he was overlooking the obvious; perhaps Nystrom didn't know anything.

But the way he'd come alive during the last few questions . . . And if Joe's theory was sound, Nystrom would figure in it. He should have left a key behind, some important misinformation that Nystrom might pass on and thus give Joe the connection.

The traffic was heavy on Sunset; he cut off of it to Doheny again and turned west on Santa Monica Boulevard. He took the Boulevard all the way to Fourth Street in Santa Monica, and then turned right.

In front of a novelty store about two doors from Sam's Shoe Salon, there was a space and Joe eased the big car into it. He put a nickel into the parking meter, which gave him an hour.

Larry Puma was standing near the doorway when Joe entered. Larry's voice was quiet. "Krivick just left. Have you eaten?"

"I had an eleven-o'clock breakfast. I can eat."

"Let's go then, while this lull lasts. If any customers come in, Sam won't let me go."

They went out and past the novelty store to a small restaurant on Arizona.

There, while they waited for their order, Larry said, "Krivick gave me the impression I was a really hot suspect. Why?"

"I don't know, Larry. What time did you leave the house this morning?"

"A little after eight. I had breakfast here and got to the store by nine. You set the alarm for eight."

Joe said thoughtfully, "I know. And you were in bed until eight?"

No delay in Larry's response and no reaction on his face. "That's right, Joe. Does that clear me?"

"I don't know. Even if Alan was killed before eight, you've no proof you were asleep until then."

"It was your house. You were there."

"Yes, but I didn't hear you get up. I slept right through to eleven."

Puma sipped his water. "So, isn't a motive necessary in a murder charge? What motive would I have?"

Joe shrugged. "None. But Krivick doesn't know that."

Puma's eyes were thoughtful. And then he smiled. "Unless it's because of last night, because you told me I'd have to find room for Alan in the new theater. But I wouldn't call that much of a motive."

"I wouldn't either," Joe agreed. "Larry, in every murder case that's tricky, or in most of that kind, somebody knows something he doesn't tell the police. Maybe it's an old scandal he doesn't want dug up. Maybe it's something unusual he witnessed that he feels the police would interpret wrong. Is there anything like that you're holding back?"

Larry shook his head. "You didn't mean my friendship with Chloe Brennan, did you? I knew her before she was a Brennan."

"I wasn't thinking of that particularly. I was thinking of the gang at the Players. You know them all pretty well, don't you?"

"Most of them. But I don't know anything about them that the police should know."

Their food came and they started to eat. Joe said, "That first was the kind of murder you should understand. It was staged. It was a theatrical presentation. I'd bet on that."

"I don't follow you, Joe."

"I don't want you to, right now. But if I'm right about it, it should practically eliminate you as a suspect."

Larry grinned. "I'd like to follow you, then. What's your theory, Joe?"

"I don't want to word it until I'm sure. But one thing these tricky killers forget is that once the gimmick is revealed, all the other suspects are more or less cleared. If you ever plan a murder, Larry, don't get cute with it."

Larry nodded. "Thank you, officer. Did you see about that house yet, that place you planned to convert for us?"

Joe shook his head. "I'll get Norah to see about it as soon as I get back to the center."

Larry grinned. "Some girl, that Norah. She'll make a great wife. She's the cream of that crop."

"I think so, too. This Metzger was pretty nasty, eh?"

Larry shrugged. "Depends on your moral standards. He had a lot of charm. Women would like him better than men would. I can stand almost anything but a phony."

"That's why you're not mourning Alan?"

Larry frowned. "I regret his death. I was drunk last night when I compared him to Metzger. Alan had a lot Dick never had. Alan was damned bright, but his theatrical knowledge was still superficial. This much I'll give him: Alan was on the right track. Dick wasn't, at least when I knew him. Maybe, as a kid, Dick was another Alan."

Joe suggested, "And maybe Bruce Dysart was, too."

"Maybe. I don't know. The man was in business. The purpose of any business is to show a profit. That includes the movie business. Within that limitation, and it *is* a limitation, you can have as much damned integrity as you can afford. You can get as arty as you want, and as subtle. But there's one error you're not permitted. You're not permitted to lose money for the firm. That's a thing, of course, the longhaired critics can't understand. It's too simple for them." He stopped and sipped his coffee. "Don't mind me; I could be wrong."

Joe smiled. "Keep talking. It makes sense to me."

"One example," Larry said. "I used to read the *New Yorker*. Until one day I read a little piece by the resigning movie critic. It was Wolcott Gibbs, I think, and he was resigning, he explained, because he discovered he was trying to review for his friends an entertainment medium designed for their cooks. Now I don't know who his friends are, but if they read the *New Yorker*, they're a rather limited group. Any movie aimed exclusively at that group couldn't possibly interest enough people to bring in a tenth of the revenue even a cheap picture needs."

"It's sort of a—oh, arty magazine, isn't it?"

"No. They have some of the finest living writers writing for them. They also have some of the worst, so long as they follow the *New Yorker* pattern. But that's beside the point. A critic who isn't broad enough to judge *any entertainment offering* within the frame of its inevitable limitations is not qualified to be a critic in that field. And if he hasn't any level of communication with cooks, I doubt if he's broad enough to judge any medium that relies on communication for its effect. That includes all the arts. And it includes the movies." Larry took a deep breath. "You asked for it."

"I enjoyed it," Joe said. "You make more sense to me than Alan did. But I'm at the cook level."

Larry rose. "And I'm at the shoe-clerk level, and Sam will be screaming. Sam thinks any young man should be able to eat in twelve minutes."

Outside, Larry said, "I don't remember if I told you last night how grateful I am for what you plan to do, Joe. If I didn't, let me say it now. I've never been more touched by anything in my life."

"Thank you. I'll see you tonight, Larry. And I'll get Norah to work on that house right away."

They were even with Joe's car now. Larry waved and went on to Sam's. Joe paused a moment, watching him, and then happened to glance toward the window of the novelty store.

The flash of bright yellow caught his eye from one of the dim corners in the dusty show window.

He walked over to the entryway to examine it more closely. On the yellow cardboard he saw the black script and realized the piece he'd found on the slope had held only half of the full name.

The name wasn't *Smith*. It was *Smithfield*.

Joe opened the door and went in.

CHAPTER ELEVEN

JOE CALLED NORAH FROM HOME and told her to get to work on that house.

"We have it listed," she told him. "I'll have them hold it until you make a payment. What—did you learn?"

"I don't know exactly. You'll be handling the lights tonight, won't you?"

"Who else? They need help in the kitchen, Joe."

"Okay. I'll help."

"They need somebody to get the coffee and the doughnuts. There's a sale on coffee at the Mayfair. And you can get the doughnuts at Bundy and Santa Monica Boulevard. That's where we usually buy them."

"I see. Hole-in-the-Head Burke, the apprentice sucker."

She chuckled. "Aren't you sorry you ever stuck your nose in that prop room door? How long ago was that?"

"A lifetime ago, and I'm not sorry. About how many doughnuts do we usually buy?"

"Seven dozen, but they ran out early last night. If we have the same kind of crowd tonight, we'll need fifteen dozen."

"We should have a bigger crowd now. Since Alan died. Well, I'll see you tonight. Take care of yourself." He hung up.

He sat by the phone and then rose and went into the bedroom Larry Puma had occupied last night. The bed was made and made well. Nobody could make a bed that well in the dark. Unless Larry had turned on the light, he hadn't left before dawn. Or could he have left for a while, and come back? Joe went to check the spring-driven alarm clock.

He had wound the alarm tightly last night; it was half unwound now. With what he'd discovered this afternoon, Larry should be more or less cleared.

Except for the coincidence of proximity, the proximity of the novelty store and Sam's Shoe Salon. But that had to be a coincidence.

Or maybe it wasn't; a person visiting Larry at the shoe store might also be attracted by that bit of yellow in the dim window.

He drove over to the Mayfair and bought six cans of coffee, regular grind. He was at the checking stand when Walter and Jean Hamilton came up behind him.

Walter asked, "Why all the crowd in front of Dysart's house this morning? Did the police discover something new?"

"Didn't you hear? It should be in the afternoon papers."

"I haven't seen an afternoon paper. What is it, Joe?"

"Alan was killed. Sergeant Krivick went over there to question him, and found him dead."

Jean asked, "When did it happen? Do they know when it happened?"

"I suppose, by now. I don't exactly. Why, Jean?"

She said quietly, "I was thinking, if it was last night, we're all clear. We were all at your party."

"It could have happened after the party," Joe told her. "It could have been any of us."

Walter asked, "Any favorites, Joe?"

Joe lied with a shake of the head. "See you tonight, folks. I'll bring the coffee and the doughnuts."

As he drove out of the parking lot, he remembered the list Krivick had asked for, the times of departure from his party. Perhaps, by now, the time of departure wasn't too important; the Department could have a more nearly accurate estimate of the time Alan had died.

At the doughnut place he had them package fifteen dozen orange, chocolate, powdered, caramel, and plain doughnuts, a dozen to a carton. He paid the girl eight dollars and twenty-five cents and made two trips, hauling them to the car.

Apprentice sucker, hauling doughnuts for an organization used as a showcase by the young and an escape from domesticity by the older. Why should he buy them a theater?

Maybe Larry Puma belonged in Sam's Shoe Salon. Maybe Leonard Smith had reached his peak as an assistant dialogue director. Maybe all of them would be better off playing their losing game, cherishing their hopeless illusions.

What had Pete Delahunt said? *Little theater for little people.*

The one he meant to give them would not be a *little* theater. A *small* theater, but not a little one. And he had faith in Larry Puma.

And he had faith in Norah Payne.

He drove past the house they'd planned to buy. It wasn't much of a house, long and narrow, but that would make a fine theater. There was a Point Realty Sign on the lawn: *For Sale—Open.* He parked.

The house was set back from the road and well shielded by shrub walls on both sides. The front lawn could be converted into a parking lot; the position of the house on the lot would prevent any undue disturbance of either neighbor. And half a block away there was a community parking lot. Of course, parking wouldn't be too much of a problem, anyway; this place was within walking distance of the shopping center.

The kitchen was adequate, with a huge window facing on the rear yard. That could be paved, and the doughnuts served from a counter built into this window.

The back yard was walled and large enough to hold an additional building that could store the props and scenery.

All the rooms were in line; the partitions could be torn down and steel beams added where they were necessary.

On the way out, Joe pulled the sign from the lawn. Maybe he was a sucker, but it was a labor he enjoyed and a communication medium he could understand.

Back at his house, he phoned Krivick, but the sergeant wasn't at the station. He left a message and went into the bathroom to turn the hot water on in the tub.

He was jumpy and itchy; he relaxed in the tub for almost half an hour. Then he put on a terry-cloth robe and went into the den to relax on the davenport. He had the record player's volume set at a minimum as he lay there, going back over everything he'd learned since that first afternoon he'd stopped at the bubbler for a drink.

He'd overlooked the obvious; this had been one of those cute ones, those tricky ones, and he'd overlooked the obvious.

Maybe because he'd wanted to. They were all his friends, one way or another. He was committed to their world now.

Did he need to be? With his money and Norah's taste, did he need to stay with these little people in their amateurs' world? No, perhaps not, but he wanted to. This much the theater offered, something for everybody, communication at all levels.

His doorbell rang, and he went to find Sergeant Krivick at the door.

The sergeant said, "I phoned in and they said you'd called, and I was in the neighborhood. What's new?"

Joe told him where he'd been and then showed him what he'd bought at the novelty store.

They were in the kitchen now, and Joe punched holes in a couple cans of beer. He brought one to the sergeant in the nook, and sat down across from him.

"Where was this novelty store?" Krivick asked.

Joe told him.

Krivick rubbed moisture from the beer can with one finger. "Right near Sam's Shoe Salon, eh?"

"Practically next door. But that doesn't implicate Larry Puma. If anything, it directs suspicion away from Larry Puma. But I'm glad I went over to see him."

Krivick nodded. "That was a stroke of luck. For me. How about Nels Nystrom? How far did you get with him?"

"Nowhere. But I probably stirred him up. You could put a tail on him now."

"On him? Why not from this end?"

"On him. And this end, too. How many men will they give you?"

"All I ask for. This is big, Joe. This is real big now. I'm going to phone the station right now, and get a man on Nystrom. You're pretty sure of him, Joe?"

"As sure as I can be without proof. His reaction was right in the pattern. Want to eat here?"

Krivick was already heading for the living-room. "I shouldn't, but I will if you're going to break out another steak."

Joe took a big steak from the refrigerator and a couple of eggs for himself. He had eaten lunch too late to be able to consume a steak.

When Krivick came back, he asked, "Why the eggs?"

"I ate lunch with Larry Puma late this afternoon. What do you think of him, Sergeant?"

Krivick settled into one corner of the nook, his back against the wall. "He seems like a pretty solid citizen. But so have some ax murderers."

"Even some politicians," Joe added. "Who are you putting on Nystrom?"

"Jess Welch. Did Nystrom get bounced from the Department or did he quit?"

"I've forgotten. If I remember right, there was some fuss about him at the time. I think he quit under a cloud, as they say."

Krivick frowned. "Strange that Dysart should hire him. He wasn't trying to save money, was he?"

Joe came over to the nook with his can of beer. "Don't ask me. Ernie, don't make any move until Nystrom does. It all adds, but how wrong we could be. And if we grabbed the wrong person, the real killer would be warned. And he'd know his only salvation would be flight. We want to be sure, Ernie. And I've a plan."

Krivick grinned at him. "Amateur dick, huh? Joe, I'll ride with you anywhere."

"Thanks. As soon as Nystrom makes a move, then. He's our finger. Could you tap his phone?"

. Krivick shook his head. "They've been on the Chief's neck about that lately. We'll have to hope a phone call won't be enough for Nels."

Joe went back to the refrigerator and took out some frozen asparagus. "We live in hope."

"I could use another beer," Krivick said. "What a day."

Joe brought him a can. There were traffic sounds outside, and the slamming of a garage door. For a moment he had a sense of being lost in time and then remembered the scene was almost a duplicate of last night's.

Krivick said, "You should charge me board. But we're closer to a solution tonight, aren't we?"

"I hope, I hope. I don't feel like cooking any potatoes, Ernie. Toast good enough with that steak? And some creamed asparagus?"

"Buttered asparagus will do for me. You get a bang out of this little theater crap, Joe?"

"I do. Do you get a bang out of that Boy Scout crap?"

"That ain't exactly crap. That serves a purpose. It makes me feel like a human being."

"So, every man to his poison, Ernie. Though I can see your point. The kids are our only hope, aren't they?"

"They're one hope. The church is another, for me. You left the church, didn't you, Joe?"

"The church left me. I couldn't swallow that double-talk."

Krivick chuckled. "Sure, you're an intellectual now. You couldn't pass the exam for lieutenant, but you know more than the priests who study all their lives."

"Lay off, Ernie. For God's sakes, don't you think I *want* to believe? And do you think believing is enough? If it is, I give you Senator McCarthy."

Krivick smiled. "A good point. Or Franco. But they'd be monsters no matter what their beliefs were."

Joe fried some bacon to go with his eggs and some mushrooms to go with Krivick's steak, then sat down to eat with the sergeant.

They didn't talk much. At last Krivick said, "Thank God you went over to see Puma today, or I'd still be working in a fog."

"Maybe we still are," Joe said. "We'd better hurry. They'll need help with the chairs again."

Delahunt and Hamilton were hauling chairs when Joe and Krivick arrived. It was going to be another SRO performance.

Joe left the rest of them before all the chairs were set up. He went out to the kitchen and filled the big enameled coffeepots. Then Jean Hamilton came in and began to arrange the doughnuts on the trays.

She told Joe, "You'd better put on a smaller pot, too. Some of our stars will want a cup before they go on. Isn't it horrible about Alan?"

Joe nodded. "I'm buying that house, Jean, the one the Players always wanted. I'm going to convert it, too."

She stared at him for a few seconds, and then came over to kiss him.

From the doorway to the prop room, Walter said, "What goes on here? Or shouldn't I know?"

"Joe's buying us a theater," Jean said. "You can kiss him, too."

Walter said nothing, but it seemed to Joe there was some moisture in his eyes. Jean said, "You'd better hurry and get made up, Walter. It's about that time."

Walter said, "I'll thank you properly when my voice comes back, Joe. God bless you."

When he and Jean were alone again, Joe said, "I'm putting Larry Puma in charge of it. How will Walter feel about that?"

"How could he? Larry's the logical director. Is he going to give it full time?"

"If he can live on peanuts."

"He can. He has, for years. It might even pay, Joe, though that's probably wishful thinking."

Then Krivick came in from the auditorium. "The joint's loaded almost. We even set up that old davenport out there. How about some of the benches from the park?"

Joe told him, "Sit down and relax, Ernie."

Then Smith came in with his make-up on and Krivick stared at him in puzzlement. "What's he, the villain?"

Smith smiled at the sergeant, and looked at Joe. "Any coffee?"

"In a second, Leonard. How are you feeling?"

"Depressed. I hear you and Norah are— Well, congratulations."

"Thank you."

When Smith went out with his coffee, Krivick said, "Just kids, aren't they? Kids, play acting. Working for merit badges. Would you make up your face like that and get up in front of a lot of people?"

"I think I would."

"For free?" Krivick shook his head. "You would like hell."

Joe laughed and brought over a couple of cups of coffee to the big table. "I'll send you a ticket when I make my debut, Ernie."

"You do that. What did he mean about Norah? Are you and the blonde engaged or something?"

"Mmmm-hmmm. I wonder if Puma is coming tonight. I want to talk to him."

"So do I," Krivick said. "I hope he's got a good memory."

Larry came just before the end of the first act. He went out into the side patio with Krivick, while Joe and Jean poured the coffee from the big pots into the smaller serving pitchers.

Then Pete Delahunt was there to help. And just before the counter got busy, Larry came back in with Krivick.

The sergeant said, "See you tomorrow, Joe. And thanks again for the dinner."

Joe waved. Larry came over to handle the lemonade. He said, "Something's going to break, is it?"

"We don't know," Joe said. "It's just a hunch I—we have."

"I see." Larry's voice was thoughtful. "You said something this afternoon about that first murder being 'theatrical.' Were you thinking of sound effects when you said that?"

Joe nodded. "Good guess. Here the mob comes. Let's go."

They sold fourteen dozen doughnuts at that intermission, and there was to be another at the end of the second act. Joe was sorry, now, that he hadn't bought more. They ran out of coffee and finished the lemonade.'

As the warning lights flashed, Larry said, "Quite a comment on the public's artistic taste. All you need to put a show over is a murder in the neighborhood."

"Maybe some of them will come back," Joe said. "At least, they know we're here, now."

They sold the last dozen doughnuts at the end of the

second act, and almost as much coffee as they had after the first act.

Larry said, "Too bad we can't take this money with us when we move."

"I thought the money belonged to the Players. We pay rent, don't we?"

"Only after ten o'clock. And the money is ours to use as long as we stay here. When we pull out, the money goes to the Park Board."

"No wonder you want your own theater. We'll bake our own doughnuts, too."

Larry grinned. "And sell French postcards in the lobby. Don't worry, Joe, we'll make it pay one way or another, won't we?"

"We'll sure as hell try. And don't you think, with a setup like that, we'll get some talent from around town?"

"I hope so. We can certainly use it."

From the direction of the stove, Sharon said, "Isn't there any coffee for the cast? There's always supposed to be coffee for the cast."

Larry said coolly, "Complain to your agent. Customers first."

Joe said quietly, "I've boiling water. I can make you some instant coffee, Sharon."

She ignored him, staring at Larry. "Our shoe clerk is in a mood again, I see. Something bothering you, Larry?"

He smiled broadly. "Not a thing. I've never been happier in my life. I've never had more reason to be happy."

Sharon's glance went from Joe to Larry and back again. Then she turned and went back to the dressing-room.

Larry said, "It's unchristian, the way I hate that woman."

Joe said nothing. He thought of a fifteen-year-old girl bedded down with Lonnie Goetz and couldn't find any room in his heart for hate.

CHAPTER TWELVE

THE CAST WAS RECEIVING CONGRATULATIONS and Joe and Larry were cleaning up the kitchen when Norah came in. She said, "The Hamiltons want to go over to Ned's for a sandwich. How about you, lover?"

"I'll go. You, Larry?"

"Payday isn't until tomorrow," Larry said. "And I have thirty-six cents to my name."

"Norah'll buy," Joe said. "She's marrying money. Who else is going?"

"Leonard. And he wants to bring Sharon."

"Don't you want him to?"

She looked at him blankly. "Why shouldn't I? What kind of remark was that?"

"I didn't want to spoil the party. If you're going to vote against bringing Sharon, I'll back you up. And so will Larry."

"And insult Leonard Smith?"

Larry said lightly, "Stop fighting, you two. Let's all be very polite to each other, just for tonight."

Norah glanced at Larry and back at Joe. "What did he mean? What's so important about tonight?"

"I don't know. I didn't say it. Ask him."

"I'm asking you, Joe. You learned something today, didn't you? From the police? Or something your investigation turned up?"

"Maybe. It's nothing I want to talk about."

"Why not?" She looked at Larry. "I saw the sergeant take you outside. Are you involved, Larry?"

"Could be. Relax, Norah. Let's not have any mysteries, now."

She stood there rigidly, glaring at Larry. Joe came over to put an arm around her shoulders. "What's the matter with you? You're not the Police Department, honey. You haven't any *right* to our information."

"I'm a human being and I have a right to know if there's a murderer in our group. I have the right to be warned against a killer, haven't I?"

Joe said quietly, "If we were certain of the killer, you wouldn't need to be warned. The killer would be in jail." He kissed her cheek. "Now, let's get this kitchen finished up and we'll all go out for a sandwich and a drink or two. Larry's right; let's be civilized tonight."

"All right." She rubbed her cheek against his. "You keep an eye on me, though, Mr. Policeman. I want protection."

Sharon came through the doorway then. "Did anyone see the scout from Paramount in the audience? I know there was one out there."

Larry smiled. "I saw him. He was leaving as I came, right before the end of the first act."

Norah said, "We should have had a stronger play. You were right about this one being weak, Sharon. Though Larry has done a beautiful job on it."

"He certainly did," Sharon agreed. "Well, I'm not personally concerned."

Larry stared at her. "What was that first sentence? Did you admit I did a good job on the play?"

She smiled at him. "I thought you did. Everyone else does, too. Friends, Larry?"

He grinned. "I can try. And now the second sentence; why aren't you personally concerned?"

"Because I've just signed up with Monarch. For *seven*

years. I'll accept your congratulations with grace." She waved airily. "I can afford to be a lady, now."

Nobody said anything for seconds. And then Norah said, "I think that's grand, Sharon. And I'm sure the others do, too. We squabble, but you were always one of ours."

"That's right," Joe said. "Congratulations, Sharon."

Larry said nothing, staring out the window at the littered patio.

"My agents just phoned me, five minutes ago," Sharon said. "Are we going to Ned's? The party's on me."

"The next party will be on you," Joe told her. "Tonight, I pay. We're celebrating the birth of our new group, with our own theater—the Dysart Memorial Theater."

Larry turned from his contemplation of the patio. "For Bruce, Joe?"

Joe shook his head. "For Alan."

"I'll get Leonard," Sharon said.

"And I'll help these boys with the rest of the cleaning," Norah said. "Come on, boys."

They were stacking the sugar bowls when Larry said, "I didn't mention it before, but I had an offer from Monarch, too, the other day. Ray Brennan's a big stockholder there."

Norah locked the cabinet and turned to face him. "And you didn't accept?"

"I didn't. I like this new idea out here, better. And besides, I've been poor all my life. I'm afraid I couldn't stand prosperity."

Leonard Smith had walked to the clubhouse; he and Sharon went to Ned's in Joe's car. Walter and Jean drove over in Sharon's and would ride back to the Palisades with Joe.

In the back seat, Leonard and Sharon talked about Monarch Films, the one firm in the industry that consistently operated in the black, even through the current TV competition.

In the front seat, Norah and Joe were quiet.

Leonard said, "What's the matter with you two? You haven't been quarreling again, have you?"

"Not in the last half hour," Norah said. "I'm sitting here, quietly envying Sharon."

"I envy her, too," Smith said, "but not quietly. What's wrong with your tongue, Joe?"

"I've been thinking of Alan Dysart," Joe said.

Smith's voice was quiet. "Don't. I thought about him all afternoon. And it didn't do me a damned bit of good. Let's think about the living, for a change."

"I'll second that," Sharon said.

In the front seat, Norah's hand came over to rest on Joe's knee.

The mood of the party at Ned's was somewhat lighter than Joe had expected. He was more familiar with violent death than any of them; it should follow that he would be less moved by it. But no one at the table seemed to be mourning Alan Dysart.

They talked of the new theater and Sharon's contract. They talked about the crowd they'd had tonight and their expectations for an audience of equal size tomorrow. For tomorrow night was Saturday night, and that was always their biggest night.

Kids, play acting, Krivick had called them. And true, to a degree. They were in a world of their own, an illusory world whose values were theatrical and whose reality came with the dawn and the time clock. They didn't want to be reminded of the time clock after an audience like tonight's.

Joe tried, but couldn't bring himself up to the general festive level. In a corner of the room, he saw a man sitting alone at a table. He didn't know his name, but he knew he worked out of the West Side Station. He was drinking a cup of coffee and reading tomorrow morning's *Times*.

A little after midnight, Pete Delahunt rose and said,

"Anyone going back to the Palisades can have a ride with me. A woman, preferably, but the offer is open to both sexes."

Walter said, "Jean and I will go with you. Unless Joe's ready to go, and Leonard? How about it?"

"I'm ready," Joe said, and looked at Leonard.

Leonard sighed. "Just when Sharon and I were doing so well. All right, I'm ready."

Joe paid the check, and they went out. Sharon lived only a few blocks away; her Chev headed up the canyon and Joe swung in a U-turn, heading back toward the ocean.

Smith said, "Sharon finally made it, didn't she? God knows she's worked for it, in her own way."

Walter said, "I wouldn't call Monarch the zenith. Have they *ever* put out a good picture?"

"Miieeoouww," Jean said.

"I'm serious," Walter protested.

Leonard said, "They never put out anything that loses money; that's more important." He paused. "To Sharon."

Jean Hamilton laughed. "If this is a crowd of money-haters, would you drop me off? I'm in the wrong company."

"I'll get out with you," Norah said. "Let us not be unduly envious tonight." She moved closer to Joe. "I've got my dream."

"Some dream," Smith said. "I've seen better faces on clocks."

Climbing Chautauqua, where Dick Metzger had died. And how many others? How many unnamed, unrecorded people of the years before there was a road here, a state here, a white man's nation?

Chautauqua to Sunset and Sunset to Bollinger to drop the Hamiltons. Leonard rode with him, and Leonard was with him when he dropped Norah off.

Norah said, "You boys are going home, aren't you? If you're not, I want to go along."

"We're going home," Joe said. "I've a hunch I'm in for a big day tomorrow." He kissed her.

The headlights of the Chrysler flashed off the apartment windows as Joe turned it around. The hundred and eighty horses under the hood murmured in the quiet night.

Smith said, "I've a feeling about something I can't analyze. Is there anything new on the murder? Or murders?"

"I'm not sure," Joe lied. "Krivick doesn't confide in me completely. After all, I'm outside the Department, now."

"I see," Smith said, and chuckled.

Joe kept his eyes on the road. "What's funny?"

"The way you lie. You haven't had much practice, have you?"

Joe said carefully, "First Norah, and now you. There must be something in the air. If you were going to guess, who would you pick as the murderer, Leonard?"

"I wouldn't guess. I wouldn't even care. Once a man is dead, what does it matter how he died?"

Joe slowed for the intersection at Via. "It matters to me. Though that might be because of my training."

"It doesn't matter to the corpse," Smith said.

"You don't know if it does or not, Leonard. Unless you've talked to corpses. You're bitter again, aren't you?"

"No. I'm sad. Because of Alan. Why couldn't it have been I? I've had a lot of years to accomplish something in. This would have been Alan's big chance."

Joe had stopped now, in front of Leonard's house. He looked over at him. "Chin up, mister. You're still alive."

In the dim light of the street lamp Leonard's smile was visible. "Yes. Yes, indeed. And perhaps, Joe, in this new theater, we can try something experimental once in a while, something decidedly *not* commercial?"

"I hope so. I think Larry will agree to that. You see, I'm just putting up the money. I haven't the background to make those decisions. But Larry, I think, is a fine, all around man. He's going to make us all happy."

Smith nodded. "You couldn't have picked a better man. Sam never really appreciated him." He chuckled. "I apologize for my sourness. I should be mature enough, now, never to feel sorry for myself. It's a quality I detest in others." He got out and turned. "Good night, Joe. I wish you and Norah all the luck in the world. You both deserve each other."

"Thank you, Leonard. And good night."

Very few houses were showing light as he came back to Via and turned toward the ocean. The houses on either side of his were dark and he turned on the light in the garage before extinguishing the car lights.

It was a gesture that shamed him, after he considered it; it had been prompted by the general uneasiness of the evening since Larry had talked to Krivick. Norah had noticed that. And who else?

He snapped off the garage light and stood there in the darkness a moment in silent rebellion against the goblins of his imagination.

He walked through the dark house to his bedroom before turning on a light. *Brave man*, he told himself. *Only thirty-four years old and no longer afraid of ghosts.*

He was emotionally and physically fatigued; he was asleep a few minutes after getting into bed.

His phone wakened him, and there was sunlight in the bedroom. He wished he'd thought of having an extension put into this room. The phone shrilled twice more before he got to it.

It was Krivick. "Nystrom made the contact last night. It seems to be the way you figured it."

"All circumstantial so far, Ernie."

"I can get a search warrant."

"And if we're wrong?"

"If we're wrong, so what? We apologize."

"And the real killer is warned and knows that we **know**

the wire is missing and the can of film. I think it would be better to go in without a search warrant, Ernie."

"You know I can't do that, Joe."

"But I can."

"Not legally, you can't. And I can't make it official for you. Nor can anybody else."

"I know."

Krivick's voice was edgy. "Listen, Joe, you're not making sense. I told you Nystrom made the contact."

"Have you ever thought that Nystrom could add two and two and get five? He knows I'm interested in somebody and he has some information on the somebody. He figures it must be worth money and he's looking for the highest bidder."

"How does that make five? That makes four to me."

"It makes four if the information he has and I want is information on the *real* killer. Nystrom thinks I know who that is, and I don't for sure."

"Well, I'm damned near sure and I don't want you to go snooping around without authority and get yourself in trouble. I'll come out. Will you be home?"

"I will. You woke me up. I'm not even dressed."

"It's eleven o'clock. What a life. Put some beer on ice."

Joe had shaved and was scrambling some eggs when Krivick came. Joe gestured toward the refrigerator. "Help yourself."

Krivick took the opened can with him to the breakfast nook. "I've been thinking about it, Joe, since I phoned, and you could be right. But do you really want to go through with it? What's in it for you?"

Joe grinned. "Don't be cynical, Ernie. I'm a citizen. Now here's the way I think we'd have the soundest case . . ."

It was a slow day. After Krivick had left, Joe cut the lawn and turned the sprinkler system on and then went in to scrub and wax the kitchen and bathroom floors. He ate lunch around three and at three-thirty, Norah phoned.

She asked, "I didn't get you out of bed, did I?"

"I've been up for hours. What's new?"

She chuckled. "The doughnuts and coffee. I—uh—wondered if you were going to handle them again tonight?"

"I won't be there tonight, honey. Think you can stand it?"

A momentary silence. "I guess. Something—important, Joe, or isn't it any of my business?"

"I'll tell you tomorrow. Or late tonight. If it's not too late before I'm through."

"Joe, is it connected with—with the Dysarts?"

"No, dear. Please don't question me."

"Joe, you're lying. I can tell. Joe—"

"Please," he interrupted. "You'll get yourself all wrought up again. Don't forget to hold that house for me. Do you want me to come down and make a deposit?"

"I'll give them my commission as deposit. I want to contribute too, Joe." A pause. "Honey, be very, very careful, won't you?"

"I will. I promise. And you be good tonight."

"I'll be waiting for your call. I'll stay up."

At four, he went to the market for groceries. He took his time but couldn't manage to use more than forty-five minutes.

He consumed another forty minutes in the barber shop and then went home to store away the groceries and beer he'd bought. It was now a quarter to seven.

He made himself a sandwich and reheated the coffee left over from lunch. He wondered if Nystrom had phoned while he was out. Nystrom wasn't obligated to tell him anything but he had also talked to Krivick, and told him nothing. If his hunch was right, Nystrom was going to be in very hot water.

At seven-thirty he phoned Krivick at home and told

him, "I'm on the way. Have a man there by ten-thirty."

"I'll be there myself," Krivick said. "I want some of the ink, if we're right. I'll check the car in the meantime."

"I want a man who can write shorthand," Joe explained.

"I can. You're not going unarmed, Joe?"

"No. See you later."

Via to Sunset and Sunset to Chautauqua and at the foot of the hill he parked in a vacant parking lot, hidden by the buildings around it from the casual viewer on the street. He walked the rest of the way.

The front door had a cylinder lock. The rear door was a duplicate of the front. He walked along the narrow porch to a high, small window and saw that it was unlatched.

The screen was a tension screen, held by three tighteners, screwed into the outer sill. The screws were loose; the screen swung free after a slight tug from the edge. He didn't make much more noise than a fire truck, worming through the small window.

He was in the bathroom and the odor of bath salts still lingered in the room. He went through to the living-room and turned on a low light in there.

There were ashes in the small, high-hearth fireplace. Joe went over to examine them and saw the small strip of Celluloid that had escaped the fire. The odor of burned Celluloid still lingered. Well, another straw, though not conclusive evidence.

There was a chance all the Celluloid was not burned; it would make an almost unmanageable fire. He put the three-inch, unburned strip in his pocket.

In the same pocket he had the yellow piece of cardboard he'd torn from his purchase at the novelty store.

He went over the apartment carefully and slowly, trying to overlook no remote place of concealment. In a two-hour search he found nothing.

He had probed the stuffed furniture, pulled all drawers completely out of their slides, examined every panel in the small den. The fireplace was open on two sides, serving both the den and the living-room. He knelt, to send the beam of his little flashlight up the dark chimney. Nothing.

There must be a garage. He went out the back door and down a flight of wooden steps. The management helped here; each garage was marked.

Under a litter of papers on a shelf at the far end of the garage, he found the film can. There was nothing in it but an empty reel. The metal tag that had identified it was missing, torn from the rivets.

He continued to search the garage and finally found, in a battered gasoline can, a tangle of chrome wire. There was no reel.

He carried the film can and the tangle of wire down to his car and locked them in the luggage compartment. Then he came back to the living-room. He put on a brighter light and stacked some records on the player and went out to see if there was any beer in the refrigerator. . . .

It was a quarter to eleven when he heard the car come in below. He sat in a huge, upholstered, armless chair, facing the door. He had a half glass of beer in his hand and some Arty Shaw on the record player.

He heard the scrape of a foot on the steps and then a pause. And then the key was turning in the lock.

When the door opened, Sharon stood there for seconds, staring at him. Anxiety at first, and then composure came to her face.

Her throaty voice: "Are you drunk? How did you get in?"

"The door wasn't locked. I walked in. I've been talking to Nels Nystrom, Sharon."

She came in a few steps and closed the door. "So have I. He threatened me. What is this, Joe, blackmail?"

He shook his head. "Murder, Sharon. You fit it like a glove."

"You're drunk. You must be drunk. Don't make a move, now; I'm phoning the police."

Joe sat quietly in the armless chair, watching her. She took two steps toward the phone, and then turned to face him. She opened her mouth, and closed it.

"I'll phone them, if you want," Joe said. "Neither one of us want them very much, though, do we?"

She came over to sit down on the long davenport, facing him. "What is the—the meaning of this, Joe? You're really not drunk?"

"On two bottles of beer? No. Cigarette?" He held up a package.

She shook her head. "Say what you have to say and then get out, Joe." Her gaze was steady on his face.

He leaned back in his chair and took a deep breath and expelled it. "All right. When Dysart was killed, you were the logical suspect. You were the *only one* in the group who knew he was coming over to the clubhouse. You were thus the only one who could intercept him at the bottom of the slope. You met him there, on the way over, and killed him."

"How could I? Joe, I was standing right next to you, when the gun went off."

He shook his head. "A .32 doesn't make that much noise. It makes a much smaller sound than that, Sharon. A .32 with a silencer makes hardly any sound at all. Who else in the Players would know about silencers?"

"You're being ridiculous, Joe. What was that noise, a backfire?"

He reached into his pocket and took out the yellow cardboard. "This is a piece of it, a little practical joker's gimmick called a *Smithfield Delayed Action Salute.* You put this into the incinerator out at the playground, after you'd killed Dysart, ditched the gun in your car, somewhere, and then came into the kitchen. If it was a new gun, you wouldn't have to worry about a paraffin test.

If it was an old gun, you could wear a glove." He put the cardboard back into his pocket. "You come into the kitchen and give us a reason for Bruce Dysart's trip to the clubhouse. Then we hear the explosion."

Sharon shook her head. "Ridiculous. And all guess-work."

"So far. Alan thought of the gimmick, and that's why he was rummaging through the incinerator. Larry tells us that you bought some shoes at Sam's the afternoon before the murder. Is that when you first saw this *Smithfield* gimmick? Or is it an old trick of Lonnie's?"

She stared at him for seconds, leaning forward on the davenport. "If you really believe all this, why haven't you taken it to the police?"

"Because," he lied, "I wouldn't want anyone to go to the gas chamber who didn't deserve it. I've sent some up there and regretted it ever since. Shall I go on?"

She nodded, staring down at her hands.

"When Alan moved in, he found the old film Bruce was saving. He probably found the record on you that Bruce had paid Nystrom to get. Bruce would go to any lengths to prevent you from marrying Alan. He threatened to ruin you in Hollywood after that last trick you pulled on *Week End Widow*. You told him to come over to the clubhouse and you and he and Alan would talk it all out. Is that right?"

"It's your story." She didn't look at him.

"I don't know what the film was about, but remembering your background, it could have been the kind of thing they show only at stags."

On the davenport, Sharon seemed to shudder visibly. She put her hands to her face.

Joe felt a faint nausea in his stomach. "Alan found the record and the film and put his pieces together and made his big mistake. He had to play detective."

Sharon said quietly, "I'll have a cigarette now."

Joe rose and gave her one, and held a light. "He had enough ham in him to relish the scene; his accusation and your denial, all recorded on the wire recorder. Adolescent, wasn't it?"

"The scene you've described is. Will you turn off that damned record player?"

Joe went over to turn it off. He turned and stood there. "Alan didn't know about Lonnie Goetz and the kind of woman who could take two years with him. He underestimated you, didn't he?"

She turned on the davenport to face him. "All of this is a theory, isn't it? You haven't any proof."

"I have your fingerprints on that cardboard. I know how to take fingerprints, Sharon. We can have you identified by the proprietor of the novelty store. He remembers a redheaded woman who bought one of these delayed action gimmicks. You aren't a girl who is easily forgotten, Sharon."

Her face was rigid. "What is your purpose in telling me all this? If you don't intend to give it to the police, why tell me about it?"

"Because I'm not going to tell the police if you can convince me the murders were justified."

"I don't believe that. This is a trap, isn't it? Someone is listening. You're trying to frighten a confession from me."

Joe walked over to the phone. "I'll get the police, then. I've enough for them, I think."

She watched him lift the phone from the cradle and start to dial. Then she said hoarsely, "Wait—"

Joe came over to sit in the armless chair again.

Sharon leaned forward to put her cigarette out. When she straightened again, she faced him calmly. "Motive I'll admit, but not the deed. I'll tell you my motives and then you can determine if the act of killing, itself, is important or not. Bruce did have a film of me. And it was the kind they show at stags, but not stags where anybody even resembling a human being would go. It was that—degraded. He did have a record that Nystrom had accumulated for him, including the two years with Lonnie. Bruce would have ruined me if I'd gone ahead and married Alan. And I meant to, before this big chance came up, at Monarch. I meant to marry Alan right up to the moment I got this contract at Monarch."

"And Alan staged that little scene in the study?"

She nodded. "He threatened me with exposure unless I admitted to the police that I had killed his uncle. I told him he was crazy, and left."

"And came back?"

"You can believe what you want about that. I'm only saying I had reason enough to kill both of them. It's motive you were looking for, isn't it? It was motive you were going to judge me on, not the act."

"As long as you've admitted as much as you have, what prevents you from admitting the act?"

She put her cigarette out in an ash tray on the long coffee table in front of the davenport. She looked at him candidly. "What I've admitted can probably be proved. But nobody saw either of them die."

"And the gun?" Joe asked. "Did you get rid of that?"

"What gun? Joe, I've told you all I mean to about the Dysarts. I'll tell you one more thing now. If you help me stay clear, you'll never regret it. I'm solid now, and there isn't anything I wouldn't do to stay that way. I'm worth it, too. You could find that out."

Joe stood up and faced the bedroom. "Get it,' Ernie? Get it all?"

From the shadows at the far end of the room, Krivick said, "I got it. Joe. Every word. Though we really didn't need it. We found the gun."

From his luggage compartment, Joe took the wire and

the can and handed them to Krivick. He said, "Ernie, if I live to be a thousand years old, I'll never forget that look Sharon gave me when she heard your voice."

Krivick shrugged. "So, I was a schtunk. We found the gun in a padded clip way up under the cowl of her car. The clip was riveted to the rear end of the glove compartment. You see, that was Lonnie's old car. He gave it to her when he left her. And it was probably one of Lonnie's guns, though it wasn't registered, naturally."

"And the gun matches, and her fingerprints were on it?"

"Right. And speaking of fingerprints, we got another fine set off that window you found open. Young Dysart's. He was really trying to play detective, wasn't he? Even suspected you."

Joe studied the sergeant. "One question, please. Why in hell, if you knew she was guilty, did you let me go through that damned farce I just finished in her apartment?"

Krivick smiled. "Oh, we knew she wasn't armed. And I've learned what a ham you are and I didn't want to cut your lines when you had such a fat part. I enjoyed every second of it, Joe."

It had started to sprinkle and Joe got into the car. "It's going to pour in a minute, Ernie. Better get back to your car."

"Sure. Luck, Joe. Be seeing you in the papers."

Joe nodded and cut down the slope to Channel. He headed toward the ocean, toward Norah's, the big tires murmuring on the wet blacktop, making small, whimpering sounds in the dark night.

Printed in the United States
By Bookmasters